Soursweet

Soursweet

screenplay by
IAN McEWAN

faber and faber
LONDON · BOSTON

First published in 1988
by Faber and Faber Limited
3 Queen Square London WC1N 3AU

Typeset by Goodfellow & Egan Limited, Cambridge
Printed in Great Britain by Richard Clay Limited, Bungay, Suffolk

British Library Cataloguing in Publication Data
McEwan, Ian, *1948*–
Soursweet.
1. English cinema films – Scripts
I. Title   II. Mo, Timothy. Sour sweet
791.43′72

ISBN 0-571-15355-0

There were times during the writing of this screenplay when I thought of Timothy Mo's novel, *Sour Sweet*, as a splendid mid-nineteenth century mansion with many well-lit, well-appointed, well-heated rooms furnished, in the custom of the period, almost to bursting point. I am the hooligan builder. The estimate is in, the job is mine. Already I have taken my sledge-hammer to the front door. Now I am in the hallway, glaring at the fittings and knobs, the dados, the ogees, the architraves. Even as a novelist, I would be suspicious. As the modernizer, the adapter, I have nothing but contempt. It's all coming out. By the time I am finished, this house will be a roofless shack. There are rooms, whole staircases to be demolished. There are characters to be evicted without mercy. As for those who remain, the ones lolling so comfortably in their elaborate surroundings, pretending to be real, they are in for a nasty surprise. Their creator, in the manner of the period, clearly believed in them. He has lovingly provided faces, gestures, inner lives. Each of these people comes with a history, a little biography, a past that seems really to have been lived. When I am through with them, these jokers will have nothing to show but what they say or do, and there won't be much of that.

To adapt for the screen a novel you admire, particularly if it is the sort of novel you could never write yourself, can feel like brutal, arrogant work. Consider the end result. You have moved effortfully from what is, or aspires to be, a work of art, a self-contained experience, the product of a single mind, to something a sixth of its length, of diminished literary content, peppered with curt, bureaucratic non-sentences (EXT. STREET. DAY) and laughable attempts at subjectivity at which the novel above all other forms excels (*Cut to* LILY's *point of view*). And you will not have written to please yourself alone. You will have taken into account what you think the director thinks he wants to shoot; you will have accommodated, in the earliest drafts at least, the producer's thoughts about how he is going to persuade the investors.

All the colour and texture the work had as a novel is gone. All the colour and texture it might one day assume as a film will be provided by director, lighting, cameraman, designer, actors, editor, composer, among many others. You are an intermediary, crossing and re-crossing the border between the two forms; your screenplay is nothing more than a set of instructions addressed mostly to strangers who are not bound to obey.

In fact, much of the pleasure as well as the craft of screenplay writing, is in devising the kinds of instructions that people will want to follow through. A novelist may play God with imaginary characters and situations. The screen-writer has a chance to play God with the real world. It takes a few seconds to type, '*Midnight.* NIGHT BROTHER *crosses the street in heavy rain*'. It is for the director and everyone else to worry about a night shoot, police permission to block off the street, the hire and operation of a reliable rain machine, overtime for the crew, a catering truck to dispense bacon rolls and coffee, accommodation nearby for the actors, duplicate sets of clothes for the drenched actor to change into for the retakes. So it is tempting for the director, who has a larger claim to being God but is more put upon than any god could reasonably expect, to delete both 'midnight' and 'heavy rain' from the script. After all, what is lost to the cause of mimesis if Night Brother crosses the street on a dry afternoon? Everything in a screenplay, therefore, has to be scrutinized, argued for, justified. The instructions need to make a great deal of sense.

There is a superficial comparison to be made here with the short story in which, it is often said, every word must count. But in screenplays words hardly count at all; the phrasing of the instructions is not an issue. All that is required is clarity, for the pages which are consulted daily throughout pre-production and shooting mark the route towards a more important raw material – the thousands of feet of film which will one day fill a whole wall of shelves in the cutting room. Structurally, however, there are similarities between short stories and screenplays. Against the eight hours it might take to read a full-length novel, a feature film's one hundred minutes already seem rather slight; its screenplay will be even slighter. It has as much writing, or typing, as a long short story of, say, thirty pages. Both forms must respond to the same exigencies; to take their worlds as given rather than pick them apart, to establish characters and their situations with economy and speed, to digress at their peril.

Because I like short fiction, and because my inclination as a writer is to compress and exclude, I take pleasure in screenplays. Timothy Mo's *Sour Sweet* is digressive and leisurely. Its characters, who themselves are carefully, lovingly unwrapped for us, cannot take for granted their world – London in the early sixties – because they are immigrants. Nor can the author, because one of his concerns is to explain Chinese life, Chinese habits of mind, to an English readership. Both the plot and the sub-plot, the struggles of the Chen family, and scheming and warfare among the Triads, are divulged methodically and without hurry. The process is almost stately. The novel is rich in social detail and background facts and, despite its tragic structure, warmly observant of the little scuffs and rubs of domestic life. The sympathy extended to the Chen family characters spills over into objects – a black plastic sofa which hisses when sat on, an old banger which Lily learns to drive, the mango plant Man Kee cultivates. Some of the best touches of humour derive from cultural misunderstanding and are subjective and therefore difficult to translate into film: Lily, whose thoughts are never far from her ancestral obligations, approves when she hears a garage mechanic exclaim in a moment of stress, 'Far kin aid her!'; she is appalled when her son, Man Kee, comes home from school and tells her that the teacher has been showing the class the Terror Pin.

By the end, the reader is likely to feel nothing but familiarity and affection for the family group, Lily, Chen, Mui and Man Kee. They are vivid on the inner eye, knowable, thoroughly understandable. *Sour Sweet* is one more example of the novel's capacity to investigate character, to provide intimate access to private states of mind, to show how difficult it is for people to understand one another and tell each other what they feel. It is easy to put the novel aside and murmur to oneself what a fine movie it would make, (if the inner eye were celluloid . . .) but in the matter of character, film is erratic and achieves the delicacy of interpretation of the novel only in its rare and finest moments.

Preserving these characters (and initially we thought mostly of Lily), providing the opportunities for actors we had not yet seen to make them as fallible and believable as Mo had done, and at the same time maintain what turned out to be a rather complex plot without losing these characters in it, to find some parallel with the warmth and wryness of Mo's narration, and to present Chinese domestic and gangland life without explaining it or obscuring it – these were the initial problems of adaptation.

The contract which sets out the terms by which a writer's services are hired is a useful guide to how many films are written. Provisions are made for a first draft, a revision to that draft and a 'polish'. There is usually a lengthy pause at this stage while the producer takes this version of the script around to see if money can be raised to make the film. If there is success, work begins on a second draft which is likely to incorporate all the major rethinks, second thoughts, sudden inspirations or failures of nerve which have come to the writer and director during the interval. There follows a set of revisions, a polish, and perhaps one more set of revisions during the final stages of pre-production, and then some last tinkering once the actors have arrived and gathered for a read-through. The process is neither as schematic nor as continuous as it sounds. In our case the 'script development' stretched over two and a half years, during which time I wrote a novel, and the director, Mike Newell, made a television film in London and a feature film in the United States.

There are countless scenes in Mo's novel with cinematic possibility and the first draft excluded very few; it illustrated the problems we would have to solve, and it provided the basis, the material, for all future versions. I no longer consulted Mo's novel. The first difficulty was the sub-plot. The Triads meet regularly to talk policy. We witness tensions between the leadership and the senior officers; we gather, little by little, information that is crucial to our understanding of the plot, to the fate of Chen, the innocent waiter who owes the Triads a 'favour'. In script form these meetings were quite unconvincing; here were Chinese bad-men telling us how bad they were and what bad things they were going to do. In all later versions of the script, the role of the Triads was successively reduced. The role of Fok, the kitchen labourer who conducts Chen to the gambling basement, was expanded so that he became the one who imparts to us, through actions rather than discussion, the information we need. Even in the cutting room, the Triad scenes continued to be reduced; however interesting and appalling organized crime might be in real life, in movies (though not, perhaps, in literary novels) it has a well-thumbed quality, and in the case of *Soursweet* might create false expectations in an audience.

By the end of the first draft we took the decision to set the film in the present. The producer, Roger Randall-Cutler, had argued that it would be difficult enough to get a British audience to identify with Chinese characters; placing them twenty-five years in the past would compound the difficulty. And valuable resources would have to be spent dressing locations. For the director and me, the decision instantly decongested the script. Lily, Chen and Mui would no longer have to be so innocent, so baffled by the culture into which they were assimilating themselves. The actors would be less tied down, there would be more space for interpretation and idiosyncrasy. The dialogue could be a little more knowing and relaxed, less comically formal. We could be freer in our use of locations, the camera could wander. There were losses too, of course. Scenes which we had become committed to and tried to adapt to the new time scheme ultimately had to go: the Chens confronting the Inland Revenue for the first time; the triumph of car ownership and Lily learning to drive after Chen had failed; Chen finding a ship through a seaside telescope and murmuring his touching speech to his son, Man Kee, about returning home one day. The differentials in wages, education and expectations generally between the New Territories and Great Britain are not as wide as they once were; paying taxes, owning a car or taking a cheap flight home would be nothing special to a modern Lily and Chen.

Numerous changes were made to the order of scenes for all kinds of reasons which are now lost to me. In fact there came a time quite early on when I could no longer distinguish between what originated from the novel and what I had added. When I took Timothy Mo to see the set in the summer of 1987 and he praised one of the scenes in the script – Mui translating for

Grandfather in front of the coffin – I was astonished, for I was certain he had written it that way himself.

By the time the producer, director and I met to discuss what was needed for a second draft, we were reasonably certain that there would be money to make a film. There were two large worries about the script. The first was that though the scenes read well enough, there seemed to be no centre, nothing holding it together. Lily was our central character, the strong young woman who is determined to survive, and yet she did not quite seem central enough. The script, the director insisted, had no heart. The second problem was the opening. Mo had cleverly compressed Lily and Mui's childhood, their work in a factory as young women, and Lily and Chen's courtship into a few pages at the beginning of the novel. We too wanted to begin in Hong Kong, but we couldn't accept three different time schemes in ten minutes, nor did we want to burden the film with flashbacks. The solution to the first problem turned out to settle the second. I proposed that the film's real subject was Lily and Chen, the marriage, their relationship, their adventure in coming to England, the clash of their different personalities. We should play up the affection between them, and also chart its decline once Fok has located Chen and is blackmailing him. Lily's loss at the end would seem all the more poignant if we were strongly aware of the love that preceded it. From all this it followed that we should start with a traditional Chinese wedding in one of the villages of the New Territories. We would be able to experience an alien culture without needing anything explained to us – everyone understands a wedding. We could establish Lily's father, the fighter who has trained her. We could see Mui, and Chen's father who will come later to live with the family in England. Above all, we would be able to set out, as it were, with the young couple, and catch up with them four years later in England.

From then on the script began to float free of the novel. It remained faithful to its spirit, I believe, but its priorities were now its own; in the first draft versions I had felt I was doing violence to a novel; now I was gradually improving upon the basis for a film. I was also writing to the clear requirements of a director who knew exactly what he wanted to shoot. This in itself was satisfying. Mike Newell found his cast in China, Taiwan, Hong Kong, New York, Los Angeles and London. As the actors arrived and read their parts through, I made some final adjustments and prepared to go abroad. The production offices were filling with strangers, people from wardrobe, design, casting, location. Everyone had a set of instructions. Work on the film was only just beginning, and it was time for me to fade out.

Ian McEwan
Oxford
January 1988

Soursweet was first shown as part of the Directors' Fortnight at the Cannes Film Festival on 14th May 1988. The cast included:

LILY	Sylvia Chang
CHEN	Danny Dun
MUI	Jodi Long
MAN KEE	Speedy Choo
RED CUDGEL	Soon-Tek Oh
WHITE PAPER FAN	William Chow
NIGHT BROTHER	Shih-Chieh King
GRANDPA	Han Tan

Casting Director	John Hubbard
Production Designer	Adrian Smith
Director of Photography	Michael Garfath
Editor	Mick Audsley
Composer	Richard Hartley
Associate Producer	Paul Cowan
Based on the novel by	Timothy Mo
Screenplay by	Ian McEwan
Producer	Roger Randall-Cutler
Director	Mike Newell

A First Film Company production

*Open country near Hong Kong. From a vantage point, we are looking
across cultivated fields at a traditional village which is set against a
backdrop of thickly wooded mountains. Lights are just beginning to
come on. There are tropical evening sounds – frogs, crickets, birds.
One or two peasants are making their way from their fields along
narrow tracks towards the village.*
    Cut to:

A dimly lit room in the village. A pretty young woman, LILY, *sits on
a wooden chair while a* GO-BETWEEN *combs her hair and recites
these traditional verses spoken to a bride on the night before her
wedding.*
GO-BETWEEN: An auspicious day fine and fair,
        Good things come in pairs.
        May you both live together till your hair is grey
        A happy long life, with blessings every day.
    Cut to:

*Brightness and noise. From an elevated position a quarter of a mile
away we are watching a wedding procession making its way along a
path between rice fields.*
    *It is a boisterous group which includes musicians, the groom and his
friends. Flag bearers bring up the rear. Faintly we hear laughter,
scraps of song, string and wind instruments, drums.*
    *The dominant colour is red, vivid against the pale green immensity
of the fields.*
    *The group makes its way along the path that connects one village
with another. They are coming to collect the bride.*
    Cut to:

LILY, *in traditional wedding dress, sits on the floor in the centre of the
main room of the house feigning an improbable grief.*
    All around her, the bridesmaids and MUI, LILY'*s unmarried older
sister, press in to comfort her. They are enjoying themselves. There are
giggles, nudges.*
    LILY'*s father,* TANG, *an old ex-fighter, wears his ordinary
working clothes. He watches the proceedings impassively.*

The GO-BETWEEN, *whom we now see is a kindly looking, matronly lady, stands to one side.*

LILY *wails, addressing her bridesmaids in turn. They answer with stagey cheerfulness.*

LILY: I'm leaving my beloved home. I'm so sad. I think I'm going to die. Send for the coffin-maker . . .

MUI: Don't cry, younger sister. You've got a little iron to freshen up your party clothes with.

LILY: How can I live away from home? When I'm dead please forget I ever existed.

(SECOND GIRL *is barely fourteen.*)

SECOND GIRL: Don't cry . . . don't . . . we'll . . . take you dancing with us and make you . . . make you happy.

(*As she fumbles, the others giggle.* LILY *bites her knuckle. The* GO-BETWEEN *frowns.*)

Cut to:

The edge of the village. Briefly, we are down among the procession. The noise is deafening. Village children run alongside. Villagers line the road to watch.

We catch sight of CHEN, *the groom, a dreamy-looking young man in a suit which does not quite fit. He is showing signs of nerves.*

All around him his chums are joking and back-slapping.

Cut to:

Lily's home. The din of the approaching procession has reached the house. The bridesmaids, shrieking with excitement, run to take up their positions by the front door.

LILY *retreats to the back of the room. She listens anxiously. The* GO-BETWEEN *touches her sleeve and smiles.*

Cut to:

The procession comes to a halt outside the front door.

Chen's BEST MAN *knocks.* CHEN *is just behind him.*

Girls' voices from inside shout, 'What do you want?'

The young men outside laugh.

BEST MAN: He's come to collect his bride.

(*The door opens. The bridesmaids block the way. The girls and boys are acutely conscious of each other.*)

2

BRIDESMAID: If you want to see her, you've got to pay.
BEST MAN: How much?
BRIDESMAID: Nine hundred and ninety-nine thousand dollars!
    (*Jeers from the boys, laughter from the girls.*)
BEST MAN: That's too much.
BRIDESMAID: How much you got?
    (*The* BEST MAN *has taken 'lucky money' – a bright red envelope
    with money inside – from his pocket.*)
BEST MAN: Nine cents!
    (*More laughter as the door slams on the young men.*)
    Cut to:

*Now the procession is double the size as it makes it way out of the
village.*
    Cut to:

Everyone is crowded into the main room of Chen's family's house.
    *Throughout this and all that follows there are camera flashes and
constant chatter.*
    The couple bow three times to the ancestral tablets.
    Cut to:

3

The couple kow tow to CHEN'S PARENTS *who sit side by side as Lily's did.*

The old man is small and wiry with a mischievous look. The old woman is old and looks ill.

The GO-BETWEEN *is ready with the tea.*

As soon as the lucky money has been handed over, the parents get up and make way for another pair of elderly relatives.

The packets of lucky money are piling up.

Cut to:

LILY *has come into the bedroom to sit on the marriage bed.*

A dozen or so children – all relatives on Chen's side – queue up noisily to be given sweets.

As soon as they have what they want, the children, encouraged by LILY, *climb on the bed and bounce and roll about and tickle each other.*

The GO-BETWEEN *and* MUI *look on approvingly. So many children on the bed is bound to bring the bride fertility.*

Cut to:

Sudden calm. An interlude in the celebrations.

In the bedroom LILY *and* CHEN *are now alone. From here they can hear the sounds of voices and kitchen clatter as the evening's banquet is prepared.*

She is on the edge of the bed, removing her shoes.

He stands by the window and looks nervously across at LILY. *Their eyes meet momentarily. Then they look away.*

Cut to:

The banquet.

A great din. Fairy lights hung from trees illuminate the scene.

There are ten circular tables with about ten guests at each. We come in midway through the evening.

The GO-BETWEEN *is supervising as plates of shrimp, chicken and pork are being brought round.*

There is lemonade, Coca-Cola, rice wine and brandy to drink. The brandy is knocked back like beer.

At the table which concerns us we find both sets of PARENTS, LILY *and* CHEN, *his* BEST MAN, *and* MUI.

4

CHEN's *diminutive father is seated next to the muscle-impacted hulk of* LILY's. *They are getting on well. They raise their glasses and down their brandy in one.*
   Cut to:

An hour later.
   CHEN *has taken a thick envelope from his pocket and is about to read from an official document. The* BEST MAN *calls for silence.*
CHEN: The Secretary of State, in exercise of the powers
      conferred by the British Nationality Act 1981, hereby grants
      this certificate of naturalization to the person named below
      who shall be a British Citizen from the date of this certificate.
      (*There are cheers.* LILY *smiles proudly up at* CHEN.)
      Cut to:

An hour later, between courses.
   The girls have drifted together. LILY *and* MUI *stand face to face playing an old game adapted from a training technique to improve a fighter's responses – slap and dodge.*
   One of the bridesmaids interrupts, takes LILY's *hand and examines it.*
   LILY *shows off the calluses along the edge of her hand to the girls.*
   Her FATHER *has come over to join in the talk. He shows the calluses on his hand.*
   Suddenly he and his daughter strike the attitudes of fighters about to engage. They hold the poses for a few seconds and begin to circle, shadow boxing. There is applause. Someone takes a picture.
   The two straighten. The FATHER *puts an affectionate hand on* LILY's *shoulder.*
   Cut to:

A hush.
   Everyone stands to watch Lily's father, TANG. *The old fighter is staring at a huge demijohn which is being held by two young men.*
   LILY *can hardly bear to look.*
   TANG *draws breath, concentrates, then shatters the demijohn with one butt of his head.*
   There is applause. One of the young men comes forward with a glass full of brandy.

LILY *goes forwards too, concerned for her father.*

TANG *sits down, raises his hand to his head and winces.* LILY *puts her hand to his head and soothes him.*

Over this private moment – everyone else is talking – superimpose title credit: SOURSWEET.

Cut to:

Towards the end of the evening.

LILY *stands and sings a simple song with guitar accompaniment.*

CHEN *watches, glazed with drink and love.*

Cut to:

It is dawn.

LILY'*s song continues.*

A long shot shows CHEN *and* LILY, *carrying suitcases, coming along a footpath between fields.*

CHEN *appears to be insisting on carrying* LILY'*s suitcase as well as his own.*

At first she refuses; he insists, and she capitulates to social form.

They continue, LILY *ahead,* CHEN *coming along behind, staggering with the double weight.*

Cut to:

As the couple arrive at a road, a bus comes into shot.

It stops, they climb on.

The bus recedes along a dusty road.

Cut to:

The Ho Ho Restaurant, Soho, London. Five years later.

An eruption into movement and noise.

We are in the kitchens at peak business.

A chit bangs down in the hatchway. We follow the high-speed assembly of a dish of beef and vegetables in oyster sauce as it passes through the hands of preparation chef, assembly chef and stir chef.

Two dozen other dishes are being put together in the same way. Hands are blurs. It is all competence, precision, and above all, speed. We glimpse pans of brightly coloured sauces, sizzling woks, mountains of noodles and rice.

6

The extractor fans roar. The chefs shout to their assistants who shout at each other. The cooks shout to the waiters who shout back through the hatch.

Thirty-five seconds after the arrival of the chit, our dish is ready. We go with it through the hatch and emerge, in one unbroken shot –

Into the main part of the restaurant. There are more than a hundred tables. The place is packed, the conversations merge to a roar. The Ho Ho is a success.

A long brisk tracking shot and we follow our dish down an aisle.

As soon as it thumps down on a table, we look round. There are waiting customers crowding a small bar by the door.

The OWNER is snapping at a BUSBOY to clear and prepare a vacated table.

Wine corks are drawn, there are bottles of champagne in ice buckets.

And food, forked and chopsticked into talking mouths, a woman picking at a crab claw with her teeth, a man carefully folding his dried duck into a pancake, fingers in a lemon water bowl.

There are customers with raised arms. 'Sizzling' dishes flash by us.

Credit cards crunch through the roller. At a vacated table littered with dirty dishes, a saucer piled with twenty and ten-pound notes.

Cut to:

Two hours later. The worst is over. Two-thirds of the tables are empty now. It is almost silent. A couple of waiters are lounging by the hatch. Another, CHEN, is idly strolling towards the street end of the restaurant, a napkin carelessly slung over his shoulder.

He pretends not to see the raised hand of a customer – a table of young men recently disgorged from the pub – and arrives behind the barbecue chef, LO.

LO works in a glass-fronted booth facing the street. He is chopping cold meat. The cleaver is a blur in his hands.

CHEN stands dreamily behind LO and, typically, makes no attempt at opening the conversation.

LO registers his presence, but goes on working. For the moment, silence between the two friends is enough.

At the sound of a loud 'Oi, you!' from the young men's table, CHEN turns and goes towards them.

Cut to:

The kitchens, an hour later.

The place is spotless, foodless, everything has been stowed, the chefs have gone home. A young boy is polishing the stainless-steel drainer by the sink.

In a corner a knot of waiters cluster about FOK, *a kitchen labourer. A little on the short side, street-wise, flash in a way that does not quite come off.*

FOK: Easy, easy. Listen, American chicks are the easiest in the world. Listen, last night, I had not one, but two. Two! A pushover. And both blondes.

(A murmur of appreciation. CHEN, *however, is not impressed.)*

WAITER: How much money did they want, Ah Fok?

(There is laughter. FOK *pretends to spit in disgust. He shakes his finger at the* WAITER.*)*

FOK: *(Dropping his voice)* What do you know about money?

(He has pulled from his back pocket a fat wad of twenties. CHEN *lets out a hiss of contempt as he passes* FOK. FOK *looks up sharply.)*

Cut to:

8

Ten minutes later. A brief moment. The waiters eat in silence, tiredly.
  Behind the diners, the empty restaurant.
  Cut to:

Another brief moment. The shot has a stylized, formal quality. CHEN
*waits alone at a suburban stop for the connecting night bus that will
take him home to his family. We are seeing him from across the street,
illuminated from above by the light of a street lamp. We sense his
patience and isolation. Nothing moves. It seems the bus will never
come.*
  Cut to:

Later the same night.
  *The Chens' home is a two-bedroom council flat on the outer reaches
of west London. The furniture is cheap and bright. A deep-pile nylon
carpet, a black plastic sofa with matching armchair in which only*
CHEN *is allowed to sit.*
  A gigantic television set dominates one corner.
  *Not far from it is the family shrine with names and pictures of
deceased relatives, and the ash of burned incense.*
  We open on LILY, *who sits at the table arranging the family
money. This keeps her occupied through the scene. She takes £200
from* CHEN's *wage packet. She slips four tenners into a registered
envelope. The same amount is placed between the pages of a building
society pass book. We see her make entries, in quick clear Chinese
ideograms in her accounts book.*
  Five years on, she is as lively and as beautiful as ever.
  MUI *sits on the sofa folding clothes and balling socks from a plastic
laundry basket. At her side is a half-read romantic novel in Cantonese.
Out of boredom, she watches an Open University programme on
television.*
  MUI, *unlike her sister, is placid and inert. Uprooted, she is
depressed. She has found no role here yet.*
  At a sound, the two young women look up. We follow their gaze.
  CHEN, *still bloated from his employee's dinner, is lowering himself
into his armchair which hisses as it takes his weight. On his lap is a
steaming bowl of broth. The gas fire hisses too and as the steam reaches
his face,* CHEN *seems to be sweating heavily already. He gives out a
sound halfway between a groan and a sigh.*

LILY *is watching* CHEN *intently.*

LILY: You don't like the soup tonight, Husband.

(CHEN *is exhausted, drained of response.*)

CHEN: 'S good.

(*He picks up his spoon wearily and drinks the soup. The sweat courses down his face in rivulets and drops into his soup. Contented,* LILY *continues her counting. She waits a moment, glances at her husband. There is no tension here. A flash of clear whites as she lifts her gaze in* CHEN's *direction. She takes a handful of bank notes and looks at them as she speaks.*)

LILY: Ah Chen, there's a new take-away counter in Burnt Oak. (*Pauses.*) Ordinary Chinese people like us with their own business.

(CHEN *mops his brow, grunts. He is barely listening.*)

The restaurant sign . . .

(MUI *stirs.*)

MUI: New Peking Dynasty Takeaway!

LILY: Sssh! The restaurant sign comes free with the Coca-Cola sign.

(CHEN *finishes his soup, belches politely, mops his brow, stands and leaves the room.*)

Cut to:

A few moments later. Since the flat has only two bedrooms, MAN
KEE*'s cot is in the hallway.* CHEN *comes to take a look at his son.*

We share CHEN*'s point of view of the child in the half-light. He is
four years old and has all but outgrown his cot.*

CHEN *stretches his hand out to caress* MAN KEE*'s head.* CHEN*'s
words are a thought murmured aloud.*

CHEN: Head's too big . . .

   Cut to:

A little later. CHEN *and* LILY *are in bed and the light is off.*

CHEN *has his back to* LILY *and is on the edge of falling asleep.*

LILY *however is awake. Her eyes catch the light and glint. She
raises herself on to an elbow and stares down at her husband. She
smiles.*

LILY: Ah Chen, you're worn out . . .

   (CHEN *grunts.*)

   Are you tired?

   (*Another grunt.*)

   . . . and how was the boss today? Did they deliver his new
car? Was he in a good mood? Or did he shout at you?
(*Between forefinger and thumb, she takes a fold of skin on*
CHEN*'s cheek below the ear and squeezes. She whispers.*)
Hey! Hey, fat boy. Wake up, fat boy. Don't go to sleep yet.
(CHEN*'s eyes open.* LILY *kisses him, reaches down under the
bedclothes and touches him. Reluctantly at first,* CHEN *assumes
his marital duties. The two lie on their sides and look at one
another.* LILY *fingers* CHEN*'s face, kisses him again.
Her kisses redouble. She guides his hands to her body. He lets
himself be carried along. Fade to:*
CHEN *lies on his back, eyes glazed.* LILY *sits astride him,
moving sinuously, a young woman with many usefully developed
little muscles.*)
Do you like this, fat boy?
(CHEN *is floating away. His eyes open fractionally, he smiles
broadly.*)

CHEN: Hakka girl . . . Wah! . . .

   Cut to:

We are close in on an aluminium briefcase.

We are in Gerrard Street, late at night. A middle-aged man in a business suit walks away from us with the case and heads towards Dansey Place.

Dansey Place is an alley which narrows towards the far end and is hemmed in on both sides by the tall backs of dilapidated Victorian buildings which now house Chinese restaurants.

The place is just wide enough to accommodate a couple of tradesmen's vehicles and a few other cars, including a large Jaguar saloon.

It has not long stopped raining. The mossy, crumbling walls are streaked with the damp from overflowing gutters. In one place water slides down the walls.

From somewhere in the alley comes the steady, echoing sound of dripping water.

The man reaches the Jaguar, pauses to make certain he is alone, and then unlocks the door.

He opens it, and is about to get in when a sound makes him straighten.

Three men come into shot and surround the first man. These are young men, conscious of their street style.

The car owner hands over the case without protest and backs off a little. One of the men makes an apologetic gesture and takes the car keys from the hand of the owner. He steps round, opens the car and starts it.

At the same time, the leader of the group, JACKIE FUNG, *a tall man, seizes the car owner by the hair and tilts his head back.*

It is at this moment we close in. The muscles in the man's face are stretched, the eyes are terrified. What happens now does so with speed. Without warning his head is driven down on to the bonnet of the car. There is a booming sound which is amplified by the chasm-like walls.

The car owner is pulled up and rammed down again.

Now his assailant pulls him clear of the wall and pins his arms behind his back. The man on the other side of the car has come round to take a flying kick.

The car owner is on the ground, unconscious.

The car is driven forwards over the unconscious man's legs. There is an audible crunch.

The car is reversed over the man's legs. This time, no sound.

A dustbin is emptied over the man's head.

A steady jet of piss cascades over his face.

We stay a moment on the half-buried victim as footsteps recede.

The three men emerge from Dansey Place into the bustle of Gerrard Street. Two men walk towards camera and are lost to us.

We keep the third, JACKIE FUNG, *who carries the case, in shot till he is lost in the crowds.*

Cut to:

NIGHT BROTHER *makes his way through the crowds on Chinese Street. He walks towards us, though a long lens denies us the sense of his progress.*

He is in his late twenties, streetwise, dedicatedly cruel. Slicked back hair, fashionably cut suit. He walks as though he owns the street.

He hails a taxi.

As it pulls into the kerb FOK *comes running up. His manner is ingratiating, self-consciously masculine. He longs to be one of the boys.*

FOK: Hey! How's business? Got anything for me?

    (NIGHT BROTHER *climbs in the taxi.* FOK *leans in.*)

    You know I can be useful.

(NIGHT BROTHER *curls his lip and slams his door shut. The taxi pulls away.*)
Cut to:

NIGHT BROTHER *strides through a busy bath-house frequented exclusively by Chinese.*

He comes to the main pool where various figures, indistinct in the steam, lounge and chat.

Among these figures he finds RED CUDGEL *towelling himself down.*

RED CUDGEL *is powerfully built. His fists seem permanently clenched. There is a scar down his back.*

Mostly RED CUDGEL *grunts non-committally. He barely registers the other man's presence.*

NIGHT BROTHER's *manner is scornfully correct.*

NIGHT BROTHER: It was worse than we thought, Elder Brother.
RED CUDGEL: Hmm.

(RED CUDGEL *moves away from the pool.* NIGHT BROTHER *keeps at his side as they pass down a corridor towards a changing room.*)

NIGHT BROTHER: Jackie Fung was cruel to let him live. They

14

pulped his skull. He's lost his sight and probably his speech.
And the legs . . . unbelievable . . .
> (RED CUDGEL *makes no response.*)

He was delivering. They took it of course. One kilo . . .

RED CUDGEL: Hmm.
> (*The younger man waits for his leader to speak. They have
> reached a changing room.* RED CUDGEL *slips on a dressing
> gown and they move off again.*)

NIGHT BROTHER: As for distribution, last month the police
picked up two of our own men.

RED CUDGEL: And?

NIGHT BROTHER: I'd like your permission to recruit
expendable runners. Not our own people. Perhaps we could
use people with gambling debts.

RED CUDGEL: Too conspicuous.
> (RED CUDGEL *pats the younger man's cheek and turns away.*)
> *Cut to:*

*The restaurant is quiet at lunch time. There is a group of young
Englishmen, faces livid with acne. They are clowning about with
chopsticks and bowls.*

  Once again, CHEN *has come to stand with his friend,* LO. *This
time he reads worriedly from a letter while* LO *works and talks.*

LO: How's Son? OK?

CHEN: Hmm . . . Good.

LO: He's a handsome little fellow.

CHEN: Mmm . . .

LO: Bad news from home, Ah Chen?
> (CHEN *stuffs the letter back into his pocket.*)

CHEN: No, er . . . good news, very good news. Everything's
fine.
> (The OWNER *appears behind* CHEN, *a few tables away.*)

OWNER: Chen!
> (*With a sigh,* CHEN *moves away towards the English group.*)
> *Cut to:*

*A long shot over a dismal scrap of playground to a high window, and
CHEN's face.*

Chen's flat.

CHEN *stares out of the window worrying about the letter he has received.*

Behind him, on the other side of the room is LILY. *She watches her husband, bemused. Finally:*

LILY: What you dreaming about, fat boy?

CHEN: Nothing.

> (*She comes up behind him.*)

LILY: Time to go to work.

CHEN: Mmm . . .

> (*Making a soft, tigerish growl, she runs her hands over his back. Suddenly she has leverage on his arm and with a shout throws him to the floor and sits astride him.* CHEN *is furious,* LILY *playful.*)

Lily! Get off me!

LILY: Kiss first . . .

> (*She kisses him.*)

CHEN: You're going to break my back one day.

> (*He submits to the kisses, warms to them, returns them.*)

It's not a wife's place to throw her husband on the floor.

LILY: It's not a husband's place to ignore his wife.

> *Cut to:*

We are looking at the family shrine – the photographs, in particular, a black-bordered studio portrait of Tang, Lily's father.

We pull back to find LILY *sitting on a chair.* MAN KEE *stands between her knees while she dresses him – lots of layers, thick winter vest, woollen shirt, sweater, tightly buttoned quilted jacket.*

LILY: When he was a young man, everyone in Kwangsi province knew his name. He was the greatest fighter of his day. Three years in a row he was champion at the tournament. He taught Mar-Mar to be a fighter too. He wanted me to be a boy, you see . . .

> (MAN KEE *smiles at such an outlandish project.*)

And at our wedding, when he was a very old man of eighty years, he smashed open a big wine jar with his head, like this – smash! . . .

> (*The boy laughs.* LILY *is looking at the photograph now.*)

. . . even though he knew he was ill and was soon going to die. So you are a very lucky boy to have such a famous grandfather, and you must always honour him in your thoughts. Now – come here, stand still – now, what are you going to do at Mrs Law's?

MAN KEE: Behave.

(LILY *smiles as she kisses his head.*)

LILY: Behave.

Cut to:

MRS LAW *is a wealthy, lonely, elderly widow. Her house is vast, opulent, tasteful.*

From out of shot, the sound of a vacuum cleaner.

A brief sequence shows that LILY *is the cleaning lady here. She vacuums, dusts the gilt round oil paintings, polishes the gold taps in the bathroom.*

Cut to:

An hour later. The living room. LILY, MAN KEE *and* MUI *take part in a small banquet, a sumptuous spread of delicacies – tarts, cakes, éclairs, Chinese sweetmeats and cuts of chicken, abalone ham and so*

on. It is served by MRS LAW's *maid,* AH JIK. MRS LAW *pours tea for them.* MAN KEE *stuffs himself with tarts.*

    LILY *is holding out her hand.*

LILY: I was telling Son all about him this morning. See, Mrs Law? Along here. It's still there.

MRS LAW: Extraordinary training for a girl.

LILY: He even taught me tiger fork technique.

MRS LAW: Not many tigers left in Hendon.

    (LILY *laughs politely. She nudges* MUI, *trying to get her to react.*)

LILY: And I'm still supple. Look!

    (LILY *springs to her feet and does the splits.* MRS LAW *turns to* MUI.)

MRS LAW: Wonderful, quite wonderful.

    (MRS LAW *is taken aback. She changes the subject.*)

    And how's your little campaign? Are you going to shift him?

    (LILY *shakes her head and smiles to herself. She and her sister hide behind their tea cups.*)

    Cut to:

The gambling basement.

    There are no gamblers. Instead new recruits have gathered to listen to RED CUDGEL.

FOK *is in the front row.*

NIGHT BROTHER *and* IRON PLANK, *another fighter, stand to one side.*

Also present is WHITE PAPER FAN. *At times we cut away to see the fastidious disapproval on his face.*

RED CUDGEL *paces as he lectures.*

RED CUDGEL: So you do well to remember our origins. We represent the old and true way, a way which has almost vanished. Now there is another more recent organization which claims the status of a Hung Society. It's called 14-K . . .

(*He pauses for effect.*)

This gang calls itself a Hung Society. But they are nothing more than criminals, thugs, street kids. Our ways are rooted in history, theirs are crude inventions. They care nothing for the ordinary decencies of life. They have no organization in our sense, but they are hungry and ambitious . . .

(RED CUDGEL *has taken out a cigarette.* FOK *is scrambling through his pockets for a lighter, but* RED CUDGEL *has his own.*)

So . . . on becoming ordinary members after initiation, you will attain 49 rank. The code, hand signs, verses and numerical system will be explained to you then . . . Now . . .

(NIGHT BROTHER *exchanges glances with* WHITE PAPER FAN.)

Leave in small groups and avoid attention.

(*The men begin to disperse.* FOK *lingers, hoping to catch* RED CUDGEL's *eye.*)

Cut to:

CHEN *is the only passenger upstairs.*

The bus makes its way along a darkened suburban street.

CHEN *is reading his letter again. His anxiety is evident. He runs his hands through his hair. His shoulders are stooped.*

Cut to:

LILY *in watchful mood. A worried* CHEN *sits at the dining table before her. She has set the nightly bowl of broth before him.*

MUI *watches late night television; the Epilogue.*

LILY *hovers over* CHEN. *The usual subject is on her mind.*

She lets him eat a couple of spoonfuls before speaking. Her tone is bright. CHEN *is on his guard.*

LILY: How's the soup tonight, Ah Chen?

> (*He nods.*)

> Not too salty?

> (*He shakes his head.*)

> You like it then?

CHEN: Yes. I like it.

> (*A continuous bleep from the television.* MUI *continues to watch hopefully.* LILY *stands at* CHEN'*s side where he cannot see her without turning round. He knows there is more to come.*)

LILY: I do so much cooking, I ought to be doing it for a living . . .

> (*He grunts.*)

> Mrs Law was saying today how Chinese people are good at business.

> (CHEN *keeps on eating.* LILY *is suddenly exasperated.*)

> Husband, we are wasting life. Let's start a business now!

CHEN: No.

LILY: Father of Man Kee! This is what we came for. We owe it to Son. You know and I know, families never stand still. They rise and fall. We've got to start . . .

CHEN: This is not the right time. No restaurant, no takeaway counter, no business. And no more talk about it!

> (*As he speaks he leaps up and snaps off the television.* MUI *stirs, blinks indignantly.*)

> *Cut to:*

CHEN *and* FOK *make their way through the bustle of Gerrard Street.*

They descend some steps to the low-ceilinged basement room which is packed to capacity.

The air is thick with cigarette smoke. Activity centres on three tables where games are being played with large dominoes.

On each of the tables, ginger is skewered by thin daggers to indicate that play is in progress.

We move through the crush with CHEN.

He stands at one of the tables watching. Players are snapping down

the dominoes with loud cracks. Money is gathered up from the table.
Men reach into their pockets for another attempt. We catch sight of a
satisfied winner stuffing a few notes into his back pocket.

   FOK *is standing close to* CHEN. *He guides him to a good place by*
the table.

FOK: Come on, Uncle. Try your luck.

   (CHEN *timidly sets down two tenners. The game is rapid, pacy.*
   CHEN *is reaching out already for his winnings – two fivers.* FOK
   is squeezing his arm.)

Uncle, you should have been bolder.

   (CHEN *puts down fifty pounds. The banker glances in* FOK's
   direction. The game begins . . . CHEN *is tense, beginning to*
   regret his wager. We watch CHEN *as much as the table. The*
   game is over – CHEN *has won a large amount. There is no time to*
   count the money – the notes are pushed in his direction and he
   gathers them up in his fist. He tries to organize the notes in his
   hands. FOK *is instantly by his ear.*)

Don't count your money, Uncle. It's unlucky and wastes
time. Keep going. Keep going.

   (*Another game is starting.* CHEN *puts down fifty again. He*
   wins.)
   Fade to:

   (*The end of another game.* CHEN *has won. He is scooping up*
   a quantity of notes. Another game is beginning.)

Let me keep your money, Uncle. I can count it for you.
Fade to:

   (*The end of the game.* CHEN *has lost. We begin a series of fades*
   to the ends of games, a sense of heady timelessness. We see CHEN
   lose twice in succession, then he wins, then he loses.)

CHEN: *How* much, Ah Fok?

FOK: Nine hundred. And with what you have in your hand there,
maybe twelve.

   (CHEN *takes some steps away from the table, ready to quit.* FOK
   stays close. We are in tight as FOK *speaks into* CHEN's *ear and*
   pushes him back to the table.)

Don't stop now, Uncle. Follow your luck through. You're a

lucky man today. The time to bid higher is when you're still lucky. And take this from me too. Go high, Uncle!
(CHEN *sets down everything he has. We end on the banker, who glances up with blank, unmoved expression as* CHEN *commits his cash.*)
Cut to:

The grubby, white-tiled men's room off the gambling room is harshly lit with fluorescent light.

CHEN *grips the sides of a wash basin, gags, then waits for the fit of nausea to pass.*

FOK *lounges by the door of one of the lavatory stalls, smoking.*

FOK: You see, your luck will change, Uncle, you see.
(CHEN *splashes his face at the basin.*)
CHEN: I'll give you the eight hundred as soon as I can.
FOK: Twelve hundred, Uncle. No need to pay straightaway.
What did you need the money for anyway?
CHEN: My father. Gambling debts, in Hong Kong. Big money.
(FOK *is tickled by this.*)
FOK: That's bad, that's really bad. There are nasty people collecting gambling debts. I'll see what I can do, Uncle. I tell you what, I know some people . . .
(CHEN *is terrified.*)
CHEN: No . . . Thank you . . . no.
FOK: Don't get the wrong idea, Uncle. These are good Chinese people who stick together to observe the old ways. Always ready to help. You know how to give face? Bring fruit, pour tea, all that old-fashioned shit?
(CHEN *knows what he is getting into here.* FOK *puts his arms round his shoulders. They walk towards the door.*)
Good. I find out for you, Uncle. Don't worry. We'll help your old man out. You see.
Cut to:

A restaurant.

CHEN *approaches the entrance clutching two bulging paper bags.*

Just inside the door are clustered a dozen or so Chinese – among them old men, women with children, a young man smoking nervously.

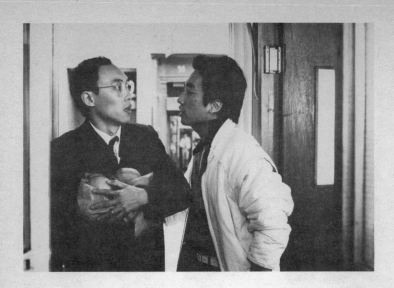

FOK, *who has taken upon himself the role of marshal, greets* CHEN *as he comes in.*

FOK: Ready? Remember what I told you.

>   (*A sobbing woman is coming from the rear of the tea house.*
>   FOK *stays the young man with the cigarette and pushes* CHEN *forwards.*
>   *We go in behind* CHEN *as he walks towards four men seated at the rear of the restaurant.*
>   *The four loook on indifferently as* CHEN *approaches.* RED CUDGEL *sits flanked by* WHITE PAPER FAN, IRON PLANK, *and* NIGHT BROTHER. *There are four empty Chinese teacups on the table.*
>   CHEN *arrives in front of the table and bows.*
>   FOK *hurries forwards with a teapot which he sets down on the table.*
>   *He hovers till a scowl from* NIGHT BROTHER *sends him away.*)

CHEN: Sirs . . .

>   (NIGHT BROTHER *stands, takes the bag off* CHEN *and shoves it under the table with his foot. He waves* CHEN *into a chair.*
>   CHEN *sits and pours tea into the thimble cups till they are half full.*

RED CUDGEL *taps the side of his cup in acknowledgement of the tribute.*)

RED CUDGEL: Our friendship association is always pleased to help those who know how to show respect. You do well to think of your father, Mr Chen. The younger generation are often forgetful of the old ways and need reminding of them. (NIGHT BROTHER *gestures to Red Cudgel's cup.* CHEN *pours another few drops into it.*)

Venerate your parents, be filial, be loyal to your friends and brothers. Your father must recover his honour, that is clear, and we will be pleased to give money for that purpose.

CHEN: Ah . . .

NIGHT BROTHER: Uncle is being most generous.

(CHEN *is being prompted. He pours more tea into all four cups.*)

CHEN: Ah . . . ah . . . you are too kind to your miserable servant, Uncle. But . . . what about the repayments . . . interest . . .

NIGHT BROTHER: Not in front of Uncle.

(*Apologetically,* CHEN *lifts the teapot. The cups are now full to brimming. The meniscus curves over the lip.* CHEN *manages to tip another couple of drops into Red Cudgel's cup. To indicate that the interview is over,* NIGHT BROTHER *stands. He shoves the bag of fruit into* CHEN'S *arms.*)

Give the fruit to your kids.

(CHEN *backs off clutching the bag.* NIGHT BROTHER *gestures down the restaurant at the waiting clients.*)

Cut to:

A few days later, after midnight.

CHEN *is walking to his bus stop from the restaurant.*

The street is empty, wet and cold. We track alongside CHEN, *letting the last scene fade, taking in the man's predicament.*

A high-angled long shot of CHEN . . . *his isolation in the empty street.*

He walks in front of Dansey Place. We are looking across CHEN'S *path, so we see it before he does – a cigarette end which glows, then fades.*

The glowing butt is sent spinning through the darkness and lands in front of CHEN.

CHEN *glances into the darkness. He has slowed, but he does not stop.*

FOK: Little Brother . . .

> (*A gasp of fear.* CHEN *hurries on.*
> *We are in the alley, watching the shapes of three men moving into the street.*)
> Colleague Chen . . .
> (CHEN *stops. His breathing is rapid.* FOK *appears flanked by two sharply dressed men. He is edgy. He is having to perform in front of the other two.* FOK *faces* CHEN *while the two men stand behind him.*)
> My friends want you to know that everything has been taken care of. Your honoured father has settled his debts. Everyone thinks highly of him again. He even has a little extra to spend on himself . . . Your relatives are all very impressed by you, very proud . . .

CHEN: Ah Fok . . .

FOK: My friends have done you a big favour, Uncle. Now we expect one in return.

CHEN: Ah Fok, you are a very kind man. I can pay you extra money, I can . . .

> (FOK's *mocking friendliness is gone. He puts his face near* CHEN's.)

FOK: Money! Who needs money? Do I look like a poor man? I didn't help you for money. That wasn't the idea. I need a favour, Uncle, a favour.

> (*In his terror* CHEN *giggles. With every 'Uncle',* FOK *shoves* CHEN *violently in the chest. The men behind* CHEN *shove him in the back.*)
> What's so funny, Uncle? You think we hang about in the dark to share jokes with you, Uncle. You think you're too important to return a favour, Uncle? Serious business, Uncle. Very serious business.

CHEN: What do you want me to do?

FOK: It'll be very easy for you . . .

> (FOK *is reaching into his pocket. In his hand are a few small plastic bags of white powder.*)
> We want some deliveries made, once a week to Sheffield.

Very simple. You can go on the train. Do it on your day off.
(CHEN *is backing away, shaking his head.*)
Think it over . . .
(*The three men retreat into the darkness from where* FOK *calls.*)
. . . get used to the idea. You'll be good at it. No one will
notice someone like you.
Cut to:

The Chens' bedroom in semi-darkness. LILY *is watching* CHEN. *She
cuddles up close to him.*
LILY: Husband . . . Chen . . . are you awake?
CHEN: Mmm.
LILY: Are you angry with me?
CHEN: No.
LILY: Is there something wrong, something you're worried about?
CHEN: No, I'm not worrying.
    (LILY *props herself up on her elbow.*)
LILY: You'll tell me, won't you, if there is. Promise.
CHEN: Promise.
    (*We have a tight shot of* CHEN. *His eyes are wide open.*)
    Cut to:

27

From a remote and elevated position we are watching CHEN *crossing an expanse of waste land – a cleared demolition site – towards some distant houses. The landscape beyond the open ground is desolate – poor housing, a few tower blocks, square miles of urban seediness. A strong wind blows.*

It is a dull, early summer afternoon. In the centre of the site a bonfire smoulders and for a moment, CHEN *is enveloped in smoke. He hurries on.*

We track alongside. He hunches himself deeper into his jacket. Under his arm he carries his copy of Dalton's Weekly.

Cut to:

The sitting room, morning. It is CHEN's *day off.*

Now that CHEN *wants to hide himself from the Triads, he wants to be converted to Lily's plan.*

LILY *is at the dining table. The paper bag of fruit that* CHEN *brought home from his meeting with the Triads is in front of her. She has taken from it a mango. Through the scene she scrapes the mango stone clean, then suspends it with toothpicks over a jamjar of water.*

CHEN *makes an awkward beginning.*

CHEN: You know, this really isn't the time . . .

(LILY *raises an eyebrow.* MUI *remains oblivious. She's watching television.*)
You know, to make a move, going into business . . .
(*The television drones.*)
I might be wrong, of course, but I think I'm right . . .
I know I'm right. We need to choose our moment . . . not rush into things . . .
(*He waits for a comeback, a defence.*)
You ought to consider these things more carefully, Mother of Man Kee. When you have a family you can't afford to take stupid risks . . . look before you leap . . . Wasting my time with these impulsive ideas . . . Really! When I'm worn out from working all day in the restaurant. Don't you think I have other things to think about? Well?
(CHEN *is thinking desperately of another approach.* LILY *gathers up the mango pulp and the paper bag and carries them out to the kitchen.* CHEN *follows her.*)
We've got all the money we need anyway.
(*He is becoming angry. Through the following* LILY'*s delight grows. By the end she is moving towards* CHEN.)
You've got all the clothes you need, Man Kee is well fed, nothing wrong with this furniture. Nothing at all! . . . We're perfectly happy as we are. Everyone envies us. Is there a better flat than this in London? We've got everything. So I don't want to hear another word about rushing to start up a business. I'm tired of listening to it. Do you hear! Not another word on the subject of starting up a business on our own and getting out of this flat and getting rich . . .
LILY: Where is it!
CHEN: (*Angrily*) Where is what?
LILY: Our new business.
(CHEN *subsides grumpily.*)
CHEN: I don't know . . .
(LILY *throws her arms around her husband's neck, and laughs.* CHEN *is torn between relief and a feeling that he has been too easily seen through.* MUI *continues to watch the Open University.*)
Cut to:

Euston station.

FOK waits by the ticket barrier. In his hand is a package wrapped in newspaper.

He glances at his watch, hesitates a moment, then stuffs the packet in his pocket and strides away towards the Underground.

Cut to:

The Chens' flat.

The living room in chaos. Two removal men are carrying away the black sofa.

LILY is packing a cardboard box with MUI's help. MUI is crying.

LILY takes MUI's hand and squeezes.

LILY turns away, and MUI privately examines her crushed fingers.

MAN KEE is under the dining table, studiously unpacking a cardboard box. We are down on his level. Beyond him, the meaningless to and fro of giant legs. At his side, his prized possession, the mango stone in its jamjar of water.

Cut to:

A moment later. MAN KEE is picked up by LILY and hugged. We see the contrast between LILY's tearful face and MAN KEE's – his interest caught by a packing case by an open window.

Cut to:

Man Kee's point of view from the top of the packing case down on to the street where a large removal van is being loaded up.

Cut to:

The removal lorry. The two removal men and CHEN stand by the cavernous rear doors.

We look in. The family possessions take up a fifth of total capacity. The removal men shrug, dust their hands, close one of the doors.

LILY is coming round the corner of the flats with a suitcase in her hand.

CHEN goes forward to meet her and take the case.

As they walk back together towards the lorry, one of the removal men shouts and points.

Everybody looks up. We look.

Out on the window sill thirty feet up, MAN KEE *is waving to them. He is leaning out too far.* LILY *screams.*

MAN KEE *loses his balance and falls.*

Everything happens at speed. We cut quickly between the various components of the scene.

CHEN, LILY *and the men start running forwards, though they are too far away to do anything.*

MUI *is just turning the corner as* MAN KEE *is about to fall. Alerted by* LILY's *scream and without taking a moment to think,* MUI *drops a case, steps forwards, stretches out her arms and catches the boy.*

Cut to:

We are tightly involved in a tangle of embraces and kisses and relieved weeping. CHEN *and* LILY *embrace* MUI *and* MAN KEE *who have rolled on to the ground.*

The child cries in shock. Faces, arms, hands, tears, kisses, comforting words, congratulations . . . The grief at moving from their familiar home which LILY *and* MUI *have been bottling up now has an acceptable outlet.*

Finally, a medium long shot of the same. The removal men stand by awkwardly, shy in the face of all this emotion, but unable to move away.

The little family group has never looked more cohesive or vulnerable as now.

Cut to:

The Chen family, installed in the back of the lorry, crouching wherever there is support. CHEN *has to stand, and fights to keep his balance as the vehicle lurches round corners.* MAN KEE *clutches his jamjar and mango stone.*

Cut to:

The lorry coming to a halt.

LILY *and* MUI *look at* CHEN *expectantly. There is a pause, the sound of footsteps round the side of the lorry, then the doors open. Fade up the din of hammering, the screech of metal, a terrible hissing.*

We are looking down the length of the lorry so that what we see is framed by the open rear doors.

31

We see a crumpled looking pre-war end-of-terrace house, with grey pebble-dash, and heavily buttressed where the rest of the terrace once was. It stands completely alone, facing across derelict land. It is separated by a road from a busy garage.

CHEN jumps down and strides towards the house with the men. The women step out more cautiously, and it is their bewildered point of view we share.

As they get down from the lorry, the din intensifies. They could be on a factory floor.

MAN KEE points towards the garage. In one corner, sparks fly. Elsewhere, men in greasy overalls lie under cars or attend to machinery. There are bits of cars everywhere.

LILY's face hardens. She turns towards the house.

MUI follows with MAN KEE carrying his mango.

Cut to:

LILY and CHEN take a tour of the house. They keep their voices low.

The narrow entrance hall has peeling wallpaper and, like the rest of the house, bare boards, some of which are missing.

LILY: Ah Chen, you've never cooked a meal in your life.

CHEN: It won't be Chinese cuisine, Lily. It's takeaway food.

32

33

It's been tried and tested. The English like it. I don't need to know anything about cooking.

(*We go from room to room, seeing cracked or crumbling plasterwork, rotten window frames, the stains of water penetration, a broken window or two. In one we find* MUI *in a state of mild shock staring at an open suitcase.*)

LILY: So out of the way. Nobody will know we are here.

CHEN: That's good! We don't want too much business at first. We have to get used to things, build up slowly.

(*We enter the bathroom. The squalor here is at its worst. The lavatory is spectacularly blocked, plaster has come away from the wall to reveal the studwork.*)

LILY: But Chen, there's no one else here.

(*We back out of the room, closing the door firmly on it.*)

CHEN: All the better. No competition.

Cut to:

LILY *comes out into the garden. It is littered with other people's discarded junk. There are broken bottles, a smashed-in lavatory, car tyres and so on.* MAN KEE *is playing here contentedly.*

She surveys this, and sighs.

Cut to:

The front room, upstairs. Mattresses have been thrown down on the bare floor. LILY *and* MUI *share a double mattress.* MAN KEE *is wedged in between them. They have covered themselves with coats and quilts.*

Light filters into the room from the garage.

We open on the three sleeping heads, the profusion of bedclothes.

Then we find CHEN. *He sits on a packing case by the window, smoking and looking down on to the street below.*

Cut to:

The same room, a different angle showing the whole family asleep. The light is grey-blue. It is dawn.

LILY *stirs. She raises her head, then, careful not to wake* MAN KEE, *she edges out of the bed.*

She has slept in her clothes. Shivering, she pulls on a thick cardigan of Chen's as she moves towards the door.
    Cut to:

Several minutes later. The light is still poor. LILY *kneels in the downstairs front room. A zinc bucket of water is at her side. With both hands clamped round a wooden scrubbing brush, she rocks backwards and forwards as she scrubs the grimy wooden floor. She sings to herself the song she sang at her wedding in Hong Kong.*
    Cut to:

A low camera, a wide angle. We look across the whole expanse of wet, scrubbed floor towards LILY. *A sense of stillness. No colour in this light.*
    The young woman squats on her haunches, barefoot, perfectly still, perfectly balanced. Only her eyes move, appraising her own work critically.
    Cut to:

The hallway. Sheets of newspaper have been spread across the floor, but wind through the open front door is blowing them about. MUI *is trying to keep them in place with her foot.*

35

LILY *comes into shot and, with her sister's help, sets about tacking the newspapers to the floor.*
Cut to:

MUI *stands on a chair in the hallway, putting the finishing touches to the hanging of a bead curtain which will prevent customers from penetrating too deeply into the house. She wears a rakish bandanna around her head.*

MAN KEE *picks up a large piece of cardboard and hands it up to his aunt.*

She tacks it up by the curtain and we read: PRIVATE. TRESPASSER WOULD BE PROSECUTED.
Cut to:

The front bedroom. LILY *is hanging out of the window, holding on to a rope. We are behind her, and cannot quite make out what she is doing, or what is on the end of the rope.*

From somewhere outside, we can make out CHEN's *voice issuing instructions.*

A medium long shot of the whole house.

LILY *is at one window,* CHEN *is at another one on the same floor. They are lowering the box-shaped illuminated sign which* CHEN *has constructed.*

They position it over the front door.

MUI *stands in foreground,* MAN KEE *at her side, indicating with expansive movements of her arm the correct height for the sign.*

The ropes are secured. The lights inside the sign come on.

We see the hand-carved Chinese ideograms and the clumsy red script: DAH LING RESTAURANT. MUI *and* MAN KEE *dance in triumph.*

And CHEN *and* LILY *are at their windows, unmistakably proud.*

Across the road the garage owner, CONSTANTINIDES, *and his mechanics look on.*
Cut to:

We are looking into the Ho Ho restaurant from across the street. LO *is in his usual position at the window.* FOK *is there too, questioning insistently.* LO *shakes his head.*

36

FOK *leaves the restaurant, glances at his watch as he hurries across the street.*

Briefly, as we follow him, we pick up LILY *coming in the other direction carrying a large parcel. A bulbous, red head protrudes.*

We lose her and go with FOK *as he disappears into the crowd.*

Cut to:

The Chens' downstairs front room, night. We are close in on Lily's purchase as it is switched on. From out of shot, the sound of wood being sawn.

There is delighted applause. It is an illuminated red Buddha, a household god. It stands about ten inches high, pot-bellied, moustachioed, scowling, bathing the room and the appreciative faces of the family in its glow.

LILY *kneels before it and spreads a sheet of newspaper on which she sets her offerings – a dish of fruit, a plate of sesame cakes, three thimble cups of wine.*

With an ornamental lighter, MUI *lights three sticks of incense and places them in front of god.*

The smoke curls up round the fearsome scowl.

LILY *takes a burned-down incense stick and rubs the soot on to her fingers.*

She makes a grab at CHEN *who is busy with his benches.*

LILY: Ah Chen, keep still . . . keep still.

CHEN: Lily! Have you gone mad?

> (*The women and* MAN KEE *are laughing gleefully.* CHEN *has acquired a sooty moustache. He enters into the spirit of the joke and lowers his face beside god and makes a ferocious scowl.*)

MUI: Brother-in-law! You are the god of us all!

> *Cut to:*

Lunchtime. LILY *goes to the glass front door and turns round the sign which announces in English that the shop is* OPEN.

She returns to the counter, takes up her position there and, of course, nothing happens.

A shifted angle suggests some time has passed. The hatch edges open. We see a pair of eyes – CHEN's *– peering out.*

The hatch slams shut.

LILY *waits.*

At the sound of someone coming through the front door, LILY
straightens, prepares herself for the very first customer.

The hatch opens. MUI *watches from the kitchen.*

*Tentative footsteps, then the head of a small West Indian boy edges
round the entrance.*

*Clutching his younger sister by one hand and a coin in the other, the
boy approaches the counter.*

*We have his point of view of its towering height. He speaks rapidly,
timidly.*

BOY: Pleasemissavyergotchangeuvafiftypeepleasemiss?

> (LILY *hears nothing but a succession of sibilants. She leans over
> the counter.*)

LILY: What you want?

> (*The boy glances about him and tries again.*)

BOY: Pleasemissavyergotchangeuvafiftypeepleasemiss?

> (*The boy is reaching on tiptoes and stretching his arm, offering his
> coin.*)

LILY: Rice? Noodles? Sweet sour pork?

MUI: He wants change. You want pennies? Buy sweets?

> (*The children nod.* LILY *rings the till, the coins are exchanged,
> the children retreat. The front door slams behind them. Silence.*
> LILY *waits.*)
>
> *Cut to:*

*The takeaway at night, the illuminated sign, and a handful of people
making their way towards the entrance.*

The kitchen.

CHEN *is working frantically to keep up with the orders. There are
five woks and four saucepans on the go.*

*We take a closer look at the food, at the woks which need constant
attention, and at the glutinous, sputtering sauces.*

CHEN *turns his back to heap rice into a tin-foil container.
Immediately, smoke begins to issue from one of the woks.*

*Pausing only to wipe the sweat from his brow, he continues to serve
up two portions of sweet and sour pork with rice.*

*We look closely at the sauce. Lighting effects heighten its iridescent
quality.*

The cartons are packed and piled.

CHEN *pushes open the hatch. Through it we glimpse* LILY's *face. As soon as the cartons are through,* CHEN *slams the hatch shut.*

We remain in the front room which is crowded with customers seated on Chen's half-completed benches in three rows, facing LILY *like a small congregation.*

West Indians, Asians, OAPs, punks, rastas, English kids – all from the nearby tower blocks.

God glowers from his corner.

LILY *hands the cartons down to a tartily-dressed twelve-year-old.*

We look at the girl with LILY. *The small face is inexpertly made up, already a little careworn, and the eyes are hard.*

LILY *attempts to make contact, but her English comes out all wrong – her tone sounds harsh.*

LILY: Hello . . . should you be home, little girl, with your parents? Aren't they worried about you?

(*The* GIRL's *eyes are narrowing in disbelief.*)

GIRL: You talking to me?

(*She snorts.*)

Chink!

(*The* GIRL *takes her food and turns her back. A friend is standing nearby.*

The GIRL *is in a huddle with her friend. There are unfriendly murmurs, open stares in* LILY's *direction, laughter. Stung,* LILY *returns the stares.*)

Cut to:

A high-angled shot establishes the Chens' shop and four juggernauts parked outside, ranged across the front of the garage forecourt.

The hiss of airbrakes, a subsiding roar as a lorry comes to rest.

Now we are looking towards the Dah Ling from inside the cab of one of the lorries.

The front door of the Chens' house opens and out comes MUI *carrying a small pile of silver-foil boxes.* MAN KEE *follows close behind with a box of his own.*

Inside the cab, the men stir. There is a low murmur of Flemish.

Still keeping the men's point of view, we watch MUI *step round the oily puddles in her slip-on house shoes.*

Now we are looking down on the two upturned faces.

40

The tin-foil cartons are handed up and money is handed down.

MUI *reaches into her apron pocket for change. A dismissive murmur
tells her that she is being tipped.*

She smiles nervously and, with MAN KEE *in tow, heads back
towards the house.*

She pauses by the gate and glances back.

Cut to:

The roar of engines, the hiss of air brakes.

*Lunch break is over. Three juggernauts are making awkward turns
in the road. We are watching from the garage forecourt, from a
position just behind the garage owner,* CONSTANTINIDES, *who
stands in an attitude of proprietorial outrage.*

He carries with him a telephone and a thick roll of telephone cable.

As one of the lorries makes its sweep round, CONSTANTINIDES *is
forced to step backwards out of the way.*

*He goes to cross the road towards the Dah Ling, but he has to let
another lorry pass.*

He strides towards the house, and we track in behind him.

We bustle into the takeaway with CONSTANTINIDES *and the first
thing we see, briefly but clearly, is* CHEN's *face framed in the kitchen
hatchway.*

41

The hatch slams shut.

MAN KEE *is on the floor with a toy.* LILY *is behind the counter
smiling nervously.* MUI *is on the customers' side doing housework.
A reverse shot shows us their point of view – a loud, huge, hairy man.
The two women look at each other. Overcome,* MUI *titters.*

CONSTANTINIDES: No, don't smile at me, dear, because I'm
   not in a laughing mood. Where's the governor?
   (*The hatch has edged open an inch.* CONSTANTINIDES *strides
   towards the hatch and jerks it open.*
   Our language convention is such that talking now to
   CONSTANTINIDES, CHEN's *English is forced, a little high-
   pitched, the tone strategically bewildered.*)
   Are you the owner?

CHEN: Owner, yes.

CONSTANTINIDES: I'd like a word, if you don't mind.
   (*There are a few terrified seconds while* CHEN *comes round from
   the kitchen when the women are left with the foreign giant.*
   LILY's *hands are trembling. She tries to occupy herself with
   stacking the silver-foil boxes.* MUI *cowers over her mop.* MAN
   KEE *stares up at the visitor with unconcealed wonder. As* CHEN
   enters, CONSTANTINIDES *extends his right hand.*)

CONSTANTINIDES: I'm Constantinides from the garage.

CHEN: Chen.

CONSTANTINIDES: I can't have you blocking my forecourt like
   that again, Mr Chen. You understand my position. You're a
   businessman yourself. Nothing personal. I've got nothing
   against nobody, but I won't stand for it.

CHEN: 'S not our fault it happens, Mr . . . Mr Con. Drivers just
   park lorries and come in here to buy dinner. We didn't want
   to be blocking your way . . .
   (MUI *breaks into a fit of giggles.* CONSTANTINIDES *turns on
   her.*)

CONSTANTINIDES: What's so funny?
   (LILY *puts herself between* CONSTANTINIDES *and her sister
   and holds up her hands.* CHEN *intervenes.*)

CHEN: Take no notice, please. Just silly girl laughing. Means
   nothing.
   Cut to:

The back garden a few moments later. MUI *is taking* MAN KEE *for a little walk.*
   Cut to:

The takeaway. The two men sit on one of CHEN'*s half-completed benches.* LILY *is serving them tea with maximum self-effacement.*
CONSTANTINIDES: I'll tell you how we can make this work for both of us, Mr Chen . . .
   (LILY *withdraws to the doorway where she watches the negotiations.* CONSTANTINIDES *has placed the phone on the bench.*)
   I want more business in my garage, you want more business in here. I'll put up one of your menus in my place and the customers can order from there. I was thinking of something like a 5 per cent commission for me. And of course I can put your phone in for you . . .
   (*He sets the cable in front of* CHEN.)
   . . . as a favour, like. You just dial the orders straight through. No trouble.
   (CHEN *has been nodding through all this.*)
CHEN: Very kind, Mr Con.

43

CONSTANTINIDES: It's a good offer.

>   (CHEN *considers, and turns in* LILY's *direction. We share*
>   CHEN's *point of view.* LILY's *face is blank. She blinks.*)

CHEN: A good offer. Yes. Agreed, yes.

>   (*The men shake hands.* CONSTANTINIDES *stands and goes to leave.*)

CONSTANTINIDES: That's settled then. I knew you Chinese
were sensible blokes. Not like those bloody West Indians.
Cut to:

Night. The garage forecourt area.

MUI *carries a pile of silver-foil cartons which she balances against
her chest. In thin slippers she makes her way across the oily concrete of
the forecourt towards a lorry.* MUI *stands on tiptoes to hand the
cartons to the driver in his cab.*

The door of the cab opens and the driver climbs down.

He pulls after him a container of Coca-Cola cans.

MUI *walks back towards the house, followed by the driver with the
container on his shoulders.*

We keep our distance as he sets the container down by the front door.

*But he does not leave her immediately. They stand close. He puts his
hand on her shoulder.*

Cut to:

*Lunchtime. The Chen family are eating in their kitchen. We come in
on quiet laughter.*

MAN KEE *listens.*

LILY: It's true! Only a few types of faces, and no expression. It's
all pink skin, like pigs, and big clumsy faces. And empty,
empty eyes.

>   (MUI *looks up sharply at* LILY.)

CHEN: When I first became a waiter, I had to remind myself that
they're not really ghosts. They're real. Like us.

MUI: Of course they are.

LILY: These young girls buying dinner when they should be at
home. No wonder they get themselves pregnant. They age so
quickly. Suddenly they're old women, nothing in between.
Funny skin.

MUI: They're not ghosts! And they're not white-skinned pigs either. Take some trouble. Look at them. Some of them have lovely eyes . . . There are lots of different kinds of faces. But you don't even look at them. You just take their money.
(*We register* LILY's *and* CHEN's *astonishment at this outburst*.)
Watch English people, younger sister! You'll see. They're not pigs. They've got feelings, just like everybody else!
Cut to:

A street in West London.
  FOK *pulls up outside a Chinese restaurant in his customized Ford Sierra.*
  A waiter is lounging in the door.
  FOK *crosses the pavement to speak to him. The waiter shrugs, shakes his head, gestures further up the street.*
  FOK *returns to his car.*
  Cut to:

A swing park.
  CHEN *pushes* MAN KEE *high on a swing. We see the delight on the father's face; now that he has left the restaurant, he is enjoying his son for the first time.*
  CHEN *twists the chains of the swing, then lets go.* MAN KEE *is spun round and round and laughs deliriously.*
  Cut to:

The Chens' front bedroom. CHEN *and* LILY *make love.* CHEN *lies on his back,* LILY *sits astride him. This time she has a blanket draped across her naked shoulders against the cold.*
  Her voice is rich with affection.
LILY: Husband, where do you and Son go to play?
(CHEN's *voice is dreamy, remote*.)
CHEN: In the park, on the swings and slides. But I don't twist him on the swing. It's dangerous . . . it could make him sick . . .
LILY: What are you talking about, fat boy? How can you twist someone on a swing?
CHEN: Doesn't matter, Lily. We don't do it anyway.

45

LILY: I want you to enjoy yourselves. But Father of Man Kee,
   promise me you won't go on the waste ground. You might
   cut yourselves on all that broken glass.
   (CHEN *is drifting away. Lay over this last line into the next scene.*)
CHEN: Don't worry . . . It's all OK . . . don't worry . . . safe
   here . . . safe . . .
   Cut to:

The kitchen, early morning. January.
   At the kitchen table LILY *is checking and packing pencils, crayons,
a rubber, a ruler – all items brand new – into a pencil box. She puts
the pencil box in a new satchel along with an apple.*
   MAN KEE, *in his best clothes, with new school blazer, stands by the
table.*
   Just beyond him is MUI *dabbing at her eyes.*
   With an air of ceremony, LILY *puts the satchel diagonally across*
MAN KEE's *shoulder and then makes ritual adjustments to his clothes.*
   Cut to:

The school is in the classic, gloomy Victorian style.
   *Children are swarming in across the playground towards the main
building. Mothers of new pupils are escorting their children across the
playground.*
   LILY *however hangs back by the school gates. She drops to one knee.*
LILY: Show me what you do when you know the answer.
   (*Obediently,* MAN KEE *raises his hand.*)
   In class you're always quiet, always watching the teacher.
   (*He nods.*)
   Now work hard, Son, be obedient, play close attention.
   Bring honour to your family, to your Mama and Papa.
   (*He turns without a word and walks alone across the playground.*
   LILY *watches him go.*)
   Cut to:

The afternoon of the same day.
   Holding hands, CHEN *and* MAN KEE *make their way through the
crowds of schoolchildren.*
   They arrive at the bus stop as a bus pulls up.
   As they are about to step on to the open platform, CHEN *glances
back down the street. He flinches.*

46

His point of view. Fifty yards away is FOK. *He stops as he recognizes* CHEN. *Then he breaks into a run.*

CHEN *yanks* MAN KEE *on to the bus which immediately begins to move off.*

CHEN *remains with his son on the rear platform, paralysed, watching helplessly through the rear window as* FOK *sprints and gains on the lumbering bus.*

MAN KEE *is oblivious.* CHEN *grips the boy's hand tighter, and draws him closer to him.*

In the bus, voices, laughter.

FOK *is within a couple of feet of the bus. His hand is stretching out to grasp the upright pole.*

For a moment he is coming no closer, then the bus puts on a little more speed and he drops back by a foot or so.

He trips and sprawls.

Cut to:

Twenty minutes later.

We are tight in on MAN KEE *who sits on one of Chen's benches.*

By him is a glass of milk, on his face, a milk moustache.

Occasionally, he blinks.

LILY: Could you understand the lessons, Son?

MUI: Did you make friends with the other children?

LILY: What did you learn? Numbers? Writing?

MUI: Were there any Chinese children?

> (*Cut to the kitchen.* CHEN *sits alone. His hands are shaking. Through the hatch we hear* LILY's *voice. Her irritation is beginning to show through.*)

LILY: Are you going to be a good boy and answer Mar-Mar? Do you want to watch television tonight? What did you do in the classroom?

> (*Cut back to the front room.* MAN KEE *mutters.*)

MAN KEE: Played.

LILY: Played? Played! What about your lessons?

MUI: Would you like a biscuit?

> (MAN KEE *shakes his head.*)

LILY: What did you have for lunch?

> (MAN KEE *intones the unfamiliar words.*)

47

MAN KEE: Mince, jam tart and custard.
> (MUI *and* LILY *look at each other.* MAN KEE *repeats the words to himself.*)
>
> Mince, jam tart and custard.
>
> (*He gets down from the bench.*)

LILY: Mince–jam–tart–and–custard?
> (*In the kitchen* MAN KEE *passes behind* CHEN. MAN KEE *opens the door and lets himself out.*)
>
> Cut to:

The kitchen, an hour later.

> LILY *is sitting at the table preparing vegetables.* MUI *is nearby, preparing to go out to the dustbins. She lifts a bag full of rubbish with a weary sigh.*
>
> *Lily looks up from her work and glances towards her sister whose back is turned.*
>
> *For the first time we and* LILY *notice that* MUI *has become fat, very large indeed. We watch* LILY'*s face move through a quick succession of expressions – mild interest, sudden concern, growing suspicion.*
>
> *As she watches,* MUI *places her hands in the small of her back and sighs.*
>
> *The size of her spreading midriff and the effort that bending costs her cause* LILY *to put down her vegetable knife and stand.*
>
> MUI *is making for the door.*

LILY: Mui! You're pregnant!
> (MUI *speeds up. With* LILY *we follow her out of the kitchen, along the hall and out into the front garden.*)
>
> Eldest Sister! . . . Ah Mui!
>
> (MUI *stops by the front gate but does not turn round.*)
>
> Do you hear me?
>
> (MUI *nods.*)
>
> Hah? . . . Are you pregnant?

MUI: I don't know.
> (LILY *has come up behind* MUI *and hisses in her ear.*)

LILY: You don't know!
> (*A lorry driver is walking out of the garage. He waves across at the women.*)

DRIVER: Hello darlings!

(LILY *seizes her sister's arm and bundles her into a car which is parked by the front gate.*)

LILY: When was your last period?

MUI: Five months.

LILY: Five! You thought you were going to keep this a secret? Mui, when did you do it? *Where* did you do it?

MUI: Do it? Do it? You're not interested in who, are you? Only where and when?

(LILY *considers. We follow her gaze towards where a couple of lorries are parked.*)

LILY: How many men did it?

(*With a little cry of exasperation,* MUI *succumbs to rage. She batters her sister with ineffectual punches.* LILY *holds her off easily enough, but she is aware of* MR CONSTANTINIDES *who is staring curiously at the sisters. As the assault fades out,* LILY *slips her hands under her sister's – an inspired revival of their childhood game of slap and dodge.*)

Come on. Mr Con is looking.

(*The women work up a rhythm before beginning their chant. They play through their tears.*)

Mui–does–the–father–know?

MUI: He–does–n't–know.

LILY: Do–you–want–to–tell–me–who?

MUI: I–do–not–want–to–tell–you.

(CONSTANTINIDES *smiles to himself and walks on.*)

LILY: As–you–like . . . it's all right, he's gone now.

(*The sisters sit crying in the car.*)

Cut to:

The takeaway.

It is the Chinese New Year. February.

The red Buddha, 'god', glows on top of the television set.

A large goldfish in a bowl is the centrepiece of an improvised altar. The takeaway counter has been covered with an embroidered tablecloth. Dishes flank the goldfish bowl – plates of fruit, savoury and sweetmeat snacks, tangerines still attached to their green leaves and stalks, lettuce leaves, red dates and monkey nuts.

Over this we hear MRS LAW's *polite exclamations.*

49

MRS LAW: How beautiful, truly beautiful. How you girls have worked hard.

(LILY *and* MUI *are overcome with pride and glee as* MRS LAW *takes in the room.* CHEN *and* MAN KEE *hang back.* LO *is also present, standing apart. Everyone is in best clothes.*)

Really! This is quite charming. Do you really carry on business in this delightful room? I can hardly believe it.

LILY: This is usually the counter where . . .

MUI: And Brother-in-law built these benches.

MRS LAW: What consummate skill!

LILY: When it's crowded they stand against the wall. I have to clean the marks off!

(*As this goes on,* CHEN *nods across the confusion at* LO *who shrugs.*)

MUI: Lily got these calendars free.

MRS LAW: How refined!

MUI: And look, Mrs Law. This is our cash till . . .

LILY: Lucky cash till . . .

MUI: It rings when you total the cash and this drawer slides out. We got it second-hand from a sweet shop, didn't we, Lily?

LILY: Then you have to push the drawer back yourself.

(MUI *gives a demonstration, ringing up 10p and meticulously adding a coin to the till's contents.* MRS LAW *has returned to the centre of the room from where she gives her carefully turned praise.*)

MRS LAW: How confidently you work such a complicated machine, Miss Tang. To be so young, and to have already such a head for business. I must wish you 'smooth sailing'.

LILY: Mrs Law, please meet my unworthy husband.

(MRS LAW *offers her hand.*)

MRS LAW: Indeed, I am deeply honoured.

CHEN: Ah! Mrs Law, please don't stand on such ceremony.

(LILY *is pushing a reluctant* MAN KEE *forwards.*)

MRS LAW: Oh, how handsome Son has grown. How tall, how strong!

CHEN: Big head.

(LILY *is furious.*)

LILY: Chen! He has the most beautiful head in the world.

MRS LAW: Indeed. You are to be congratulated. It is most
exquisitely proportioned.
(*End on* LILY's *'so there!' look at* CHEN.)
Cut to:

*Half an hour later. The three women take tea and talk in a huddle.
Expressions are serious.* MRS LAW *nods sagely. There are glances to*
MUI's *midriff.*
MUI *smiles, half ashamed, half proud.*
Cut to:

The same time. The two men and MAN KEE *have wandered out into
the garden.*
*There is a thin scattering of snow on the ground. A chilly wind
blows. All three are dressed for indoors.*
LO *has a bottle of brandy.* CHEN *holds out the glasses.*
CHEN: Remy Martin, hah? That's first-class brandy, Ah Lo.
LO: No need to tell me, colleague. Now, ready? Yum Sing!
CHEN: Yum Sing!
(*The men empty their glasses in one gulp.*)
Wah! French brandy, is it, Ah Lo?
(LO *is pouring again.*)
LO: French.
CHEN: They know their business.
LO: No mistake. You've got to get it down quickly to do it
justice. Yum Sing!
CHEN: Yum Sing!
(LILY *is calling to them passionately from the house.*)
LILY: Chen! Come indoors at once. That boy'll freeze to death.
Son, come here.
(MAN KEE *hugs his father's side.* CHEN *guides* LO *back to the
house, moving, however, with face-saving slowness.* CHEN *tries
to sound casual.*)
CHEN: How are things at the restaurant?
(LO *laughs.*)
LO: The same.
CHEN: Anyone ever mention me, ask after me?
(LO *giggles.*)
LO: Don't think so . . .

CHEN: Fok still there?
   (LO *shakes his head.*)
LO: Nasty type.
   (*They are about to enter the house.* CHEN *stops* LO.)
CHEN: Ah Lo, don't mention you've seen me, OK. Don't tell anyone where I am.
LO: What's the matter, Ah Chen? You owe the boss money?
   (LO *bursts out laughing.* CHEN *lets this pass with a shrug.* LO *puts his hand on* CHEN's *arm as they pass into the house and out of shot.*)
   I won't tell. I won't say a thing . . .
   Cut to:

The evening of the same day.
   An establishing shot shows three cars arriving outside a Chinese restaurant.
   A group of men makes its way towards the restaurant.
   We track fast into the restaurant. There is just time to take in the sight of about twenty men at two tables at the height of their New Year's feast.
   Then a thud as the leading man strikes a diner.
   Diners on both sides dive for cover. The men coming up from behind the camera attack them with knives.
   A cleaver hits a man scrambling for cover.
   FOK *presses himself against the wall in terror.*
   Now we see IRON PLANK *and* RED CUDGEL *advancing through the fray, intent on finding the leader,* JACKIE FUNG.
   A close-up indicates the important man. Unlike his companions, JACKIE FUNG *remains seated, watching the assault, calculating.*
   As RED CUDGEL *reaches the second table he swings with his flail and knocks two men from their seats.*
   RED CUDGEL *glances across the floor to where* IRON PLANK *too is converging on* JACKIE FUNG.
   An inexperienced attacker lunges awkwardly across the table at the seated JACKIE FUNG *who moves slightly to one side to avoid the blade and at the same time brings his fist sharply upwards on to the man's chin.*
   He takes the cleaver away from the reeling man.

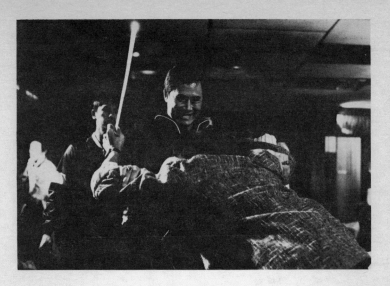

With the cleaver in his hand, JACKIE FUNG *kicks over the table.*
IRON PLANK *and* RED CUDGEL *move in closer.*
An attacker makes a broad sweep towards JACKIE FUNG *with a cleaver. He tilts his head away from the blow, but the leading edge of the steel slices across his forehead.*
Blood from the wound is blinding him.
RED CUDGEL *now moves in to finish off the wounded man. Two of Jackie Fung's own men are suddenly at his side to defend him.*
Police sirens sound.
RED CUDGEL: Finish. It's finished. Get the wounded out.
Cut to:

A private hospital. Two hours after the attack.
We are in a ward with four beds whose occupants are severely wounded and are receiving attention.
RED CUDGEL *and* IRON PLANK *are talking to one of the wounded.*
WHITE PAPER FAN *stands to one side, waiting.*
The three men come away from the bed. RED CUDGEL *is at* WHITE PAPER FAN's *side.*
WHITE PAPER FAN: Not exactly a success . . .

RED CUDGEL: We hit them hard, so let's not start calling it a defeat.

(*They are heading for the door.*)

WHITE PAPER FAN: Of course, if we have in fact eliminated their leadership . . .

(FOK *is holding open the door as they pass through. He is carrying Red Cudgel's coat folded over his arm.*)

RED CUDGEL: Who can tell? A man stands up and I kill him.

(*They pause momentarily in the reception area. As* WHITE PAPER FAN *speaks he is passing a thick envelope to a senior-looking doctor.* FOK *hovers.*)

WHITE PAPER FAN: Unfortunately, we now have open warfare. This can only be bad for business. All business.

(*They set off down the corridor.* FOK *goes after* RED CUDGEL *and offers him the coat. He is ignored. He follows the leadership as it makes its way towards the lift.* NIGHT BROTHER *registers him and scowls.*)

Worse, the authorities are going to be interested . . .

RED CUDGEL: I had to get my men out of there.

WHITE PAPER FAN: Naturally, I am not criticizing your leadership, merely indicating the situation before us. I take it we need not fear immediate retaliation.

RED CUDGEL: Correct.

(*They wait for the lift.*)

WHITE PAPER FAN: Then I suggest we build up our strength by concentrating on welfare activities. The fighters are receiving the best medical treatment and there will be cash compensations too. We should make all this generally known. As for the business . . .

(*The lift arrives.* WHITE PAPER FAN *politely hands* RED CUDGEL *in.* NIGHT BROTHER *blocks* FOK's *way. The door slides shut on him. As the leaders descend, they are aware of the clatter of* FOK's *shoes on the stairs.*)

I am concerned about the quality of some of the new recruits.

RED CUDGEL: He's recruited useful couriers for us. A waiter we lent money to who's now on a weekly run to Sheffield. And there are others.

(FOK *arrives at the ground floor as the lift doors are opening.*

54

Again, he tries to interest RED CUDGEL *in the coat.* RED
CUDGEL *takes it without acknowledgement.*)
WHITE PAPER FAN: Of course, I do not presume to
    command . . .
    (*The group arrives at the main doors.* RED CUDGEL *and*
    WHITE PAPER FAN *pass through. As* FOK *approaches,*
    NIGHT BROTHER *lets the door swing back hard in his face.*)
    Cut to:

The takeaway.
    The family has gathered in front of the ancestral tablets by the
household shrine. Prominently displayed is a photograph of CHEN's
mother. A bowl of fruit stands next to this.
    Watched by the rest of the family, CHEN *pours three thimble cups of*
tea.
    He lights three sticks of incense.
    The family bows towards the shrine.
    Cut to:

A little later the same day.
    In the aftermath of the news of the death of Chen's mother, the
family takes a day off.
    We see MUI *turning the* CLOSED *sign on the front door. She hurries*
towards a car where the rest of the family is waiting. CHEN *is at the*
wheel.
    Cut to:

Margate.
    A long shot shows the CHEN *family group walking along the*
deserted promenade. It is still early morning, and awful weather. A
wet wind blows off a grey sea.
    We note the signs of mourning – for LILY *and* MUI, *white cotton*
flowers are worn in the hair. For CHEN *and* MAN KEE, *tiny pieces of*
black ribbon pinned to the lapel.
    MUI *is noticeably pregnant now.*
    LILY *glances across at* CHEN. *He's sunk in sadness.*
LILY: Your mother led an honourable life, Husband.
CHEN: She always wanted to see her grandson. Now she never will.
    Cut to:

55

The family wanders along another part of the seafront. MUI is eating from a bag of chips. Old people sit silently in the municipal shelters facing out to sea.

MUI: But Sister, the English don't like too many foreigners here. Don't forget, he's an old man, an extra mouth to feed. The laws are very strict and they might say no.
(*She holds up a particularly fat chip.*)
You know, we could do these.

LILY: He's an old man and he has the right to come here and eat as much as he wants and be honoured by his daughter-in-law and grandson who he's never seen! Just because the English can't look after their own old people, that doesn't mean we can't look after ours!

CHEN: Lily, don't shout at sister-in-law. She doesn't make the laws. We'll see what we can arrange.
(*LILY sighs angrily.*)
Cut to:

A few minutes later.
   Leaving MAN KEE and his aunt on the promenade, CHEN and LILY have descended the stone steps to the beach.

The grey sea crashes, the pebbles rattle harshly. There are streaks of tar. It is utterly uninviting.

LILY *picks something up and goes forward to stand at* CHEN's *side. This is their first moment of leisure, first time alone outside the house in many months, years perhaps.*

LILY: I've got a present for you. Close your eyes, hold out your hand.

(She presses a pebble into his hand and closes his fingers round it.)

CHEN: Thank you. Where did you find such a beautiful thing?

LILY: My secret.

CHEN: A precious stone. I am a very lucky man.

Cut to:

The takeaway. Business as usual.

LILY: *(Calling through the hatch)* Sweet and sour chips twice.

*(*MUI *tips the chips out of a basket into tin-foil containers and passes them to* CHEN. *We are in close to see the iridescent sauce being ladled over the chips. As* CHEN *shoves the containers towards the hatch, the phone rings.* CHEN *is smiling to himself as he picks up the receiver. We watch the smile fade. He listens, nods, tries to speak but cannot make a sound.* MUI *is at the sink, her back to him.* CHEN *manages a whispered 'yes' and replaces the receiver. He stands still for a moment.* MUI *speaks without turning round.)*

MUI: Garage?

*(*CHEN *clears his throat.)*

CHEN: Yes.

Cut to:

Several minutes later. FOK *is dragging* CHEN *by the hair to where his car is parked under the railway arches.*

He releases him when he has him trapped against a wall. He smacks CHEN *about the head and face to the rhythm of his words.*

FOK: You think you can run away, Uncle? When you borrowed money? You think everyone is going to forget about you? What you going to do, Uncle? Eh? I'll tell you. You're going to pay it back. To me.

We cut, mid-stroke, to:

It is mid-afternoon and MAN KEE, *satchel on shoulder, has just
returned from school. He enters the narrow hallway and sees a large
suitcase and a strapped-up box.*

*Coming from the front room is a high female voice singing scalded-
cat style, accompanied by a full Chinese orchestra. A Cantonese opera
is reaching a climax.*

MAN KEE *approaches the door to the front room and peers in.*

GRANDPA *squats on one of the pews reading a newspaper. We see
a wizened, mischievous face, a shaved skull. His black trousers are
rolled up to his knees. His legs are tucked under him and his knees are
drawn up almost level with his ears. His elbows are spread out. To the
child he resembles a giant cricket.*

*At his side is an old Dansette record player. The record comes to an
end and, through what follows, the needle scratches and clicks in an
uneven rhythm.*

GRANDPA *looks up. He raises a scrawny finger and beckons* MAN
KEE *towards him.*

MAN KEE *stands in front of the old man who reaches forward and
finds a penny in the boy's ear.*

MAN KEE *smiles.* GRANDPA *draws a penny out of* MAN KEE's
other ear, then another from his mouth.

*He shows three pennies in his open palm, then he makes them
disappear.*

MAN KEE: Why have you got two watches?

> (*The old man pulls him closer so that he – and we – can see the
> watch faces. He speaks manically, immensely pleased with his
> own cunning.*)

GRANDPA: See! Look! Top watch tells Hong Kong time, bottom
watch tells English time. Understand?

> (MAN KEE *does not.*)

When I want to know what my old friends in the village are
doing, I look at my top watch. Ten o'clock they eat fried
dough sticks and pink rice congee with boiled soft bone
fragments. One o'clock they eat steamed pork buns and fried
beef noodle. Four o'clock they start playing mah-jeuk, drink
tea, smoke cigarettes, eat melon seeds. Dinner with snake
and tiger bone wine at eight o'clock, ten o'clock gambling
begins again . . .

(LILY *has come in on this recitation.*)

LILY: Well?

    (GRANDPA *squeezes* MAN KEE's *upper arms.*)

GRANDPA: A handsome boy! My word he's a handsome boy!
    Look at that head. It's enormous!

    (LILY *manages to keep smiling. She strokes her son's head*
    affectionately.)

LILY: It *is* a big head.

GRANDPA: Plenty of brains in there. Give him lots of fish heads,
    and chicken heads too. He'll be rich, a big businessman.

    (LILY *is pleased.*)

LILY: Worthless boy. He'll bring ruin on his parents . . .

    Cut to:

The front of the takeaway. A taxi has drawn up. MRS LAW *stands by*
one of its open doors.

    MUI *embraces* MAN KEE. *She is tearful.*

    LILY *embraces and kisses her a little frostily.*

    CHEN *embraces her affectionately.*

    A solicitous MRS LAW *helps her into the back seat.*

    The taxi draws away.

    Cut to:

Dawn. The front room upstairs.

    LILY *is just stirring.* CHEN *sleeps undisturbed.*

    What has woken LILY *is the sound of a full orchestra, a high*
female voice in scalded-cat style . . .

    Cut to:

Yawning, LILY *descends the stairs in her dressing-gown.*

    Cut to:

The front room downstairs. The music is coming from under the
counter. LILY *bends to look.*

    GRANDPA *has made his bedroom here. He lies under the counter on*
the blankets, the record player at his side. Facing him, wearing striped
English pyjamas, is MAN KEE.

    They are deep in conversation which we cannot hear for the music.

    Cut to:

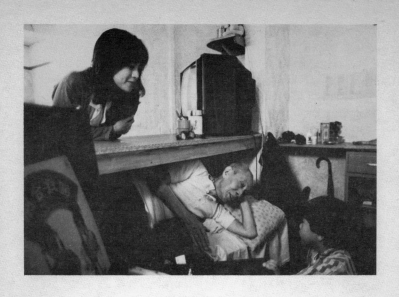

The Chens' car comes to a halt outside a modern community centre.
MAN KEE *remains in the car, his face pressed to the window watching as his mother helps* GRANDPA *towards the centre.*
Cut to:

The entrance of a large room in the community centre where twenty or so old people are gathered for an afternoon's Over-65s' Club.
Leathery heads are raised, faces crease into smiles of recognition. There's a small cheer. An old lady waves 'Cooee!'
GRANDPA *returns the wave like visiting royalty. There are appreciative murmurs.* GRANDPA *has made his mark here.*
He goes forwards, beaming goodwill.
Cut to:

CHEN *is alone in the kitchen, cooking.*
The phone rings.
He picks it up, listens, nods slowly.
CHEN: Yes.
Cut to:

CHEN *walks by Constantinides' garage. Parked a little way ahead of him is Fok's car.*

We remain at a distance as CHEN *goes forward to talk to* FOK *who remains in the car and out of shot.*

We have the impression of an argument. We see FOK's *hand make an angry gesture.*

CHEN *hands over money.*

A ringed finger is shaken at him in warning.

Cut to:

MAN KEE's *school.*

Playtime. A long lens, and a whirl of children, running, chasing, scattering before us . . . and then we make out MAN KEE *standing with two Asian boys.*

MAN KEE's *point of view through the noisy confusion. A group of tough-looking kids – two West Indians, two whites – are walking purposefully towards him.*

A reverse shows us MAN KEE *and his two friends. They flinch, but they do not move. They know what is coming.*

Cut to:

A bus stop on the main road not far from the Chens'. It is late afternoon, GRANDPA *waits for his grandson. He squats on the pavement with his back to a wall smoking, implacably patient.*

A bus approaches. GRANDPA *stands. The bus sweeps by.*

He takes up his position again.

A dissolve suggests passing time. A little figure is appearing in the distance.

GRANDPA *goes towards* MAN KEE, *puts his arm round his shoulder. They walk away.* MAN KEE *is crying.*

Cut to:

The kitchen. MAN KEE *sits on a chair under a bare light bulb.* LILY *is treating his ear which is red and swollen.*

LILY *bites her lip.* CHEN *looks on unhappily.*

GRANDPA *is muttering.*

GRANDPA: Bad boys . . . bad boys . . . bad boys . . .

Cut to:

61

CHEN *is at the bottom of the garden hoeing. He rests from his work and looks back towards the house.*

GRANDPA *squats with his back to the wall of the house watching the lesson* LILY *is giving* MAN KEE.

She delivers it with intensity. We are close in on hands. LILY *holds* MAN KEE's, *curls the fingers against the palm and places his thumb outside.*

LILY: I want you to imagine it is my father who is speaking to you now. This is a fist, Son.

(*She unwraps the hand.*)

Now do it yourself . . . No, thumb outside. There, good boy. Now the other hand . . . clever boy. Now stand sideways to Mar-Mar. Feet there and there . . . bend knees a little . . . tuck your fist under your armpit . . . no, here, thumb side on top . . . and stick your left arm out . . . leave the other one where it is. And now, slowly stick it out here, and turn the wrist over as you give fist . . . now do it fast . . . right, now hit Mar-Mar's hand.

(MAN KEE *swings wildly.*)

Good, again . . . good, again . . . now other hand, good. Now I'll show you how to kick. We use the edge of the foot, aim for shin or knee cap, OK? Go forwards when you kick, not backwards, all right. Hold this hand in front of your face when you kick to stop bad boy's fist . . . there . . .

(MAN KEE *lashes out with his foot and connects loudly with* LILY's *shin. She suppresses her reaction. She is determined to put the accident to profitable use. We cut to* GRANDPA *quietly laughing behind his cigarette.*)

Honour the memory of your grandfather. If someone hurts you, Son, *never* show it on your face . . .

Cut to:

The gambling basement.

A couple of fighters are bundling FOK *through the crowd towards a back room.*

Cut to:

The back room.

62

NIGHT BROTHER *lounges against the wall, sceptical, bemused.*
WHITE PAPER FAN *is there.*
The fighters bring FOK *into the room. He is sweaty, nervous.*
RED CUDGEL: Well?
FOK: I can't believe it. He's not there. He left suddenly. Nobody knows where . . .
RED CUDGEL: How much did he take?
NIGHT BROTHER: I checked with Sheffield. In six months perhaps as much as two hundred grams short weight.
(RED CUDGEL *brings his fist down on the table.*)
RED CUDGEL: A non-member! A miserable runner!
NIGHT BROTHER: It shouldn't be hard to find him.
RED CUDGEL: I'm making this man's death your personal responsibility . . .
(*Glances are exchanged among the others.*)
Find this man and wash him. Do it properly.
(WHITE PAPER FAN *is cool, precise.*)
WHITE PAPER FAN: A little more investigation might be appropriate . . .
RED CUDGEL: Hah! Might it? Are you the leader here?
WHITE PAPER FAN: When you recruit widely in the way you have here, problems arise. Problems of quality.
(*This reference to* FOK *makes* NIGHT BROTHER *grin broadly.* RED CUDGEL *comes to where* WHITE PAPER FAN *is sitting, puts his face near the older man's and shouts.*)
RED CUDGEL: Enough!
(WHITE PAPER FAN *is unruffled. He returns* RED CUDGEL's *stare.*)
Cut to:

Soho, late at night.
   NIGHT BROTHER *emerges from the Ho Ho restaurant into pouring rain and hurries along Gerrard Street.*
   Cut to:

He raps on the window of White Paper Fan's travel agency.
   White Paper Fan's video monitor shows us NIGHT BROTHER.
   Cut to:

The travel agency.

WHITE PAPER FAN *is at his desk,* NIGHT BROTHER *sits before him, sipping Scotch.*

NIGHT BROTHER: It's as we thought. I spoke to the owner at the Ho Ho. That runner left months ago, without giving notice. That man Fok must have been dealing the stuff himself.

WHITE PAPER FAN: It's always the same. No doubt he's been putting the squeeze on the waiter too.

NIGHT BROTHER: No point tracking him down if he's innocent.

WHITE PAPER FAN: Well . . . You are still under the leader's orders. Should there be a . . . miscarriage of justice, he'll be responsible. It's a trifling error, but it could be useful to us . . . an additional factor.

(WHITE PAPER FAN *indicates the Scotch bottle.* NIGHT BROTHER *refills.*)

. . . Now, to more immediate business. Can I rely on you?

NIGHT BROTHER: Of course. And I speak for the other side as well.

WHITE PAPER FAN: Good. Don't be confused by irrelevant loyalties. In a successful business one is sometimes forced to make redundancies . . .

Cut to:

JACKIE FUNG *has just parked his car on the corner of Dansey Place and Gerrard Street. He turns to find* NIGHT BROTHER *waiting for him.*

They set off down the street. JACKIE FUNG *limps noticeably.*

NIGHT BROTHER: Act within the agreed limits. If you kill him you'll force us into full-scale war.

(*The other man does not reply. They have stopped outside the entrance to the gambling basement.* NIGHT BROTHER *touches* JACKIE FUNG *on the arm.*)

Do you hear me, my friend? It's easy enough for you to go in here, but we could make it harder for you to come out . . . understand?

(JACKIE FUNG *nods.*)

You know the signal.

(NIGHT BROTHER *enters the basement.* JACKIE FUNG
remains on the pavement.)
Cut to:

The gambling basement.
   *It is late. We are looking across the littered floor towards the tables.
There are fewer punters now. One table is wrapping up. Punters are
leaving. The two other games are progressing desultorily.*
   NIGHT BROTHER *crosses the floor.*
   He parts the curtain.
   RED CUDGEL *is tucking into a large bowl of noodles.*
NIGHT BROTHER: Everything's in order, Elder Brother.
RED CUDGEL: The takings are in the safe?
NIGHT BROTHER: The men have just reported to me . . .
RED CUDGEL: I told you to check it yourself. Now do it! Then
   come back here.
   (*Now* NIGHT BROTHER *quickly recrosses the floor of the
   basement. He speaks to four men who are lounging near the exit.*)
NIGHT BROTHER: You're all needed across the road.
   (*The men leave. As soon as they are gone,* JACKIE FUNG *enters.*
   NIGHT BROTHER *indicates the curtained annexe.*)
   Cut to:

The curtain is ripped away.
   RED CUDGEL *is holding the bowl of noodles to his face, using
chopsticks to push the food into his mouth.*
   JACKIE FUNG *has drawn a pump-action shotgun from inside his
coat. He hits* RED CUDGEL *across the face with the butt.* RED
CUDGEL *is knocked to the floor. The bowl shatters, the food scatters.*
   JACKIE FUNG *kicks him hard.*
   RED CUDGEL *has rolled on to the open floor of the basement, and
is lying on his back, still conscious. He watches his assailant.*
   *Men at the table look on amazed. A man with a domino holds it
mid-air.*
   JACKIE FUNG *releases the safety mechanism and jacks a round
into the breech with a rich, oily sound.*
JACKIE FUNG: Come on, Uncle. Try something. How about a
   leg sweep?

(*He fires at* RED CUDGEL's *left foot – a tremendous sound.*
JACKIE FUNG *works the mechanism again. He fires at the other
foot.* RED CUDGEL *is rolling on his side, hissing with pain.*
JACKIE FUNG *hurries away.*)
Cut to:

The takeaway.
   The kitchen. MAN KEE *is just back from school. He sits at the
kitchen table, his uneaten snack in front of him. He is on the edge of
tears. His answers to* LILY's *interrogations are barely audible. He
cannot look at his mother.*
   There is a large graze on his forehead.
   LILY *questions furiously.* CHEN *looks on unhappily.*
LILY: Trouble with the teacher? Is that it?
   (*A snuffle from* MAN KEE.)
   Because you hit a bad boy and made his nose bleed?
MAN KEE: And a bad girl . . .
LILY: They hit you first! Why is teacher angry?
   (MAN KEE *sniffs loudly.*)
MAN KEE: Teacher says I do 'dirty fighting'.
LILY: Dirty?
MAN KEE: Teacher says only a coward kicks in the leg and hits
   with the head.
LILY: Hah?
MAN KEE: Teacher says it's 'dirty fighting'.
   (LILY *turns to* CHEN.)
LILY: What does she mean, 'dirty'?
CHEN: Unfair.
   (LILY *is astounded.*)
LILY: Unfair? Unfair? What's fair about fighting? The whole
   idea is to win. It's an insult to the way of the fist . . .
   (CHEN's *patience snaps.*)
CHEN: Look! Look at this! You made this happen. You filled his
   head with your stupid nonsense and he got hit again, even
   harder. The way of the fist! You think it's an honourable
   tradition. You know nothing about the real world. People are
   pushed around, and hurt, sometimes they get killed. My son
   is having nothing to do with it. Nothing! You'll keep your

66

stupid fantasies to yourself. Do you understand!
(LILY *backs off.*)
Cut to:

We are looking across the street from the Chens' house where we find
NIGHT BROTHER *smoking and lounging with his weight on one*
foot.
    He saunters across the road.
    NIGHT BROTHER *goes to one of the windows of the house and*
peers in.
    He comes round the side of the house and looks over the fence into
the back garden.
    He sees CHEN *crouching down uprooting winter potatoes.*
    MAN KEE *is tending his mango plant.*
    Nearer the house, GRANDPA *is planing wood.*
    Satisfied, NIGHT BROTHER *recrosses the road and walks towards*
his car, tossing his half-smoked cigarette as he goes.
    Cut to:

Mrs Law's.
    LILY *is in the hallway looking through to the living room where*
MRS LAW *is lovingly cradling Mui's baby.*
    MUI *appears in shot. She takes the baby, kisses it, then hands it*
back to MRS LAW.
    MUI *picks up a suitcase and carries it out of the living room.*
    LILY'*s tone is aggrieved, but she is constrained in someone else's*
house. MUI *is on the edge of tears.*
LILY: You can bring it home! It can share Man Kee's room . . .
MUI: She.
LILY: Chen says it . . . she is welcome in our house . . .
MUI: It's better for her to stay here. Mrs Law has been very
    kind.
LILY: Man Kee isn't good enough to share with Niece?
    (*The sisters watch* MRS LAW *as she walks the baby up and*
    down.)
MUI: Don't talk like that, Lily. She's a girl – a maggot in the rice.
    You have a son. There's no place for a girl in your family. I
    want the best life for her. (*She drops her voice.*) Don't you

understand what I'm telling you? Mrs Law is rich, and she's
kind. She's also lonely.

(LILY *considers a moment, then tries another tack.*)

LILY: But it's your baby. Don't you want to be with her? Aren't
you going to miss her?

(MUI *turns away.*)

MUI: Yes. I want to be with her. I'm going to miss her.

(*There is silence, sadness.*)

I want to be with her.

(MUI's *simple admission disarms* LILY.)

LILY: I'm sorry . . . I'm sorry . . .

(*She comes to her sister and they embrace, warmly. The two girls
are tearful. For what follows they remain in the embrace.*)

But why didn't you want me to see her?

MUI: I don't know . . . Lily, the father is from Belgium.

Cut to:

The Chens' garden.

  GRANDPA *sits on a large object which is obscured from view by old
sacks. Wood chippings are everywhere. He is rolling a cigarette. We
do not see who he is talking to.*

GRANDPA: This is my new country . . . also my last country. No more different places. This is where the old man dies. So, it's lucky to honour my English hosts and say thank you for taking in a weak old man from Hong Kong.
Cut to:

The family is at supper.
LILY: Where are we going to find a pig? How are you going to teach the Westerners mah jeuk?
GRANDPA: Who needs a pig or mah jeuk? Just a little to eat and drink. Everyone will be happy, you see.
MUI: No one will understand you.
GRANDPA: No need, no need! We're old. We've seen it all. There's no need for talk.
(*The girls shrug. Duty demands they honour* GRANDPA's *request for a feast for his new friends.*)
LILY: What are we going to give them to eat?
MUI: (*Shaking her head*) Old English people don't like Chinese food. Even *real* Chinese food.
MAN KEE: Mince, jam tart and custard!
(*The women turn to look at him.*)
Cut to:

A week later.
The front room. A long trestle table has been covered with sheets and laid for lunch.
The guests are all seated. Plates of mashed potato and grey mince are being distributed.
Conversation is beginning to establish itself.
GRANDPA *presides, smiling benignly to himself and smoking. He does not eat. He leans forward and pats the hand of the old man sitting close to him. The two old men exchange smiles.*
CONSTANTINIDES *and a few of the garage hands stand along the wall eating enormous portions of jam tart and custard and chatting to the voluntary workers.*
CONSTANTINIDES *gestures to* LILY *with a heaped spoon.*
CONSTANTINIDES: Lovely grub, Lily.
(GRANDPA *has left his seat and is murmuring in* LILY's *ear.*)

GRANDPA: Tell my English friends it's time to go out into garden now. I've got something to show them.

LILY: What is it? You can tell me now.

(*But* GRANDPA *smiles and turns away.*)

Cut to:

Moments later. LILY *and* MUI *are ushering the old folk out of the room towards the back garden.*

LILY *is helping an old lady with a stick towards the door.*

LILY: Come into garden, please. Something very special for you to look at.

Cut to:

The garden.

The thing GRANDPA *has been constructing is large and leans against the wall. It is covered with sacks.*

He limps up and down beside it waiting for the last of the old people to come into the yard.

GRANDPA *wants to make a speech.* MUI *stands at his side and acts as translator. He mutters his lines into her ears, she calls hers out to the crowd.*

GRANDPA: Say welcome to my foreign devil friends.

MUI: Honourable friends, welcome!

(*There is applause.*)

GRANDPA: Say, they are not here to eat food and drink tea and use the toilet, but for a very important purpose.

MUI: Ah . . . we hope you enjoyed the banquet.

(*There is a murmur of assent.*)

GRANDPA: Say, we are all very, very old, weak people who will not live much longer.

MUI: And . . . we wish you long life!

(*More applause.*)

GRANDPA: Some of us might die tomorrow . . .

MUI: Ah . . . *very* long life.

GRANDPA: Tell them, it's time to start making arrangements for death.

MUI: Grandpa! . . . We hope you all come again soon.

GRANDPA: Tell them, I am a carpenter. I have built something
they will all be needing . . .
(GRANDPA, *with a self-important flourish, pulls the sacks
away.* MUI *has her back to him and continues to translate into a
stunned silence.*)
MUI: Grandpa is a carpenter and he has made something
specially for all of you . . . and hopes it will be useful . . .
(MUI *turns.* LILY *covers her face with her hands. Propped
against the wall is a coffin and coffin lid in smooth unvarnished
wood. Undeterrred,* GRANDPA *continues his speech into* MUI's
ear.)
GRANDPA: Tell them, it's very good wood, very good wood . . .
(*There is a gathering hum of protest, anger, fear.* GRANDPA *goes
forward and takes the sleeve of an old man in the front row. He
tries to entice him nearer the coffin, pointing at the man and then
at the coffin to indicate an appropriate fit. He's grinning
encouragingly. The flock is edging away, and now is moving as
one towards the house.* GRANDPA *continues to pluck at sleeves,
trying to pull some of the other old people towards the coffin.*)
Don't be shy . . . don't be shy.
(*The old lady whom* LILY *helped starts to sing 'Abide with me'.
There is now a general move towards the house.* GRANDPA
*stands by his coffin, genuinely astonished that no one is taking up
his offer. We end on* CHEN. *He stares at the coffin, possessed by
a foreboding.*)
Cut to:

The garden.
  It is dusk, the same day.
  CHEN *has come out into the garden to be alone to think. He is
staring at the coffin propped against the wall.*
  *We see him from behind, from the point of view of someone who is
quietly coming up behind him.*
  An arm slips round CHEN's *neck and tightens.*
  An agonized 'No!' escapes him. He spins round.
  It is LILY, *laughing.*
CHEN: What are you doing! You think that's funny? Why can't
you leave me alone? You think I don't need some peace?

(LILY's *laughter dies.*)
Stupid girl! Stupid, stupid!
(*He turns and walks towards the house.*)
Cut to:

CHEN *and* LILY *are in bed. The light is low.*

  LILY *has never looked more beautiful than she does now. She murmurs soothingly to* CHEN. *She is determined to make it up to him, and to get through to him.*

  She pulls him towards her, covering his face with kisses.

  For a moment it seems they are making love, for CHEN *is on top of her.*

  His body is shaking. LILY *is caressing his head.*

  Then CHEN *rolls away from her. He presses his face into the sheet and weeps.*

  LILY *leans over him and touches his arm. She whispers.*

LILY: Ah Chen . . . my big boy, what is it, what is it? You can
  tell me . . . please tell me . . .
  Cut to:

LILY *is before the family shrine. She lights incense, and pours tea.*

  She stares at the photographs: her father, Chen's mother, herself and Chen as an engaged couple, shots from the wedding, Man Kee as a baby . . .

  Now her attention has settled on a picture of herself and Man Kee taken when he was two. The boy sits contentedly on his mother's lap. Chen stands by her proudly. She studies the photograph, gauging the changes to her life.

  Cut to:

CHEN *and* MAN KEE *are working in the garden.*

  LILY *comes towards them excitedly from the house.*

LILY: Chen! Chen! The Chinese school has just phoned. There's
  room now for Man Kee. We can take him there next
  Saturday and he can start straight away . . .
  (CHEN *is already shaking his head.*)
  What?
CHEN: No.
LILY: Why not?

(CHEN *has resumed his digging.*)

CHEN: I don't want him or you or any of us going into Soho.

LILY: But tell me why not.

(*She has come to stand close to him. Her mood is dangerous.*
CHEN *shrugs.*)

CHEN: Because I don't want it.

LILY: Is this it? No? Nothing? Don't want to? Are you ever
going to speak to me again? More than three words? Did we
come all this way to start a business so you could turn into
a vegetable, so that you could spend every spare moment in
the garden, so that you could turn my son into a peasant,
a coolie . . .

(*She has seized the nearest thing to hand which is Man Kee's
mango plant, now about two feet high. She pulls on it as she
shouts. It is hard to uproot. It comes up with a tearing sound.
Sobbing,* LILY *runs back towards the house. End on* MAN KEE,
impassive, uncomprehending.)
Cut to:

*We are close in on a child's hand setting the mango plant down on a
wooden surface. Then the lowering of a cover takes the screen to black
and then to:*

A long shot shows MAN KEE *and his father pushing the coffin on a set
of old pram wheels over the waste ground towards a large bonfire in its
centre.*
Cut to:

Drawn by the smoke, LILY *has made her way to the waste ground.*
    Ahead of her she can see the fire and CHEN *and* MAN KEE *beside
it.*
    *The ground is rough and she makes her way with difficulty in her
house slippers.*
    Cut to:

The fire. CHEN *and* MAN KEE *stand side by side. In the heart of the
blaze is the coffin. The sound of crackling wood is loud.*
    We stare with CHEN *into the flames.*

We are aware of a figure on the other side of the fire.

Through the flames wrapping round the coffin, through the smoke and heat-warp, there is no mistaking the features of NIGHT BROTHER.

CHEN's *face tightens. He makes no attempt to move away. He finds his son's hand.*

LILY *arrives at* MAN KEE's *side and puts her hand on his arm.*

LILY: We could have planted it again.

(MAN KEE *jerks his arm away.*)

Step back a little, Son. It's dangerous.

(*As the coffin is consumed, the fire intensifies.*

CHEN *turns to* LILY *and speaks with unfamiliar urgency.*)

CHEN: Lily. Take Man Kee and go home, quickly.

LILY: Chen, what is happening to you?

(CHEN *disengages* MAN KEE's *hand and pushes the boy towards his mother.*)

CHEN: Don't talk to me. Do what I say. Go! Quickly. I'll explain. Please go.

(*There is a hopeless longing in* CHEN's *look.* LILY *picks up on the desperation in his voice.*)

LILY: Come on, Son.

77

(*The boy struggles ineffectually. We watch her go from* CHEN's *point of view which we hold for several seconds. As he is pulled along,* MAN KEE *twists round to look back at his father. Chen looks through the flames to the figure.* NIGHT BROTHER *has not moved, yet.*)
Cut to:

A restaurant in Soho.
   It is well after midnight and the restaurant is closed.
   RED CUDGEL *swings on his crutches across the darkened*
restaurant. *The others are already seated and waiting for him.*
   It is a long and humiliating walk.
   The faces turned towards him are without sympathy.
   He lowers himself in his seat and glares round the table. NIGHT
BROTHER *immediately pours tea for him in the traditional,*
subservient manner. Throughout the scene he continues to top up the
cup.
WHITE PAPER FAN: I trust you are feeling somewhat better.
RED CUDGEL: Let's begin. The attack on me was an outrage, an
      insult to our society. Everybody knows it. There is now open
      warfare between ourselves and Jackie Fung. We win, or
      we're finished.
NIGHT BROTHER: That is not how we see it. They knew exactly
      who they wanted. We heard it from Jackie Fung himself.
      They were only interested in you.
RED CUDGEL: Going behind my back to talk to . . . What's
      happened to discipline here?
NIGHT BROTHER: No one went behind your back. You were in
      hospital, severely injured. It would have been dangerous for
      us to talk to you.
RED CUDGEL: An attack on me is an attack on our society!
WHITE PAPER FAN: The family Hung does not wish to get
      involved in a pointless war through the folly and arrogance of
      an individual.
RED CUDGEL: Do you know what you're saying?
WHITE PAPER FAN: To speak bluntly, what use is a crippled
      enforcer . . .?
      (RED CUDGEL *makes a movement, as if to lunge at* WHITE

78

PAPER FAN. *He falls back helplessly into his chair. His cup is refilled.*)
My friend, you no longer have the ability to manage the situations you create.

IRON PLANK: Let's not be harsh. Elder Brother deserves our respect. Before he leaves the country for higher office, we must honour him.
(RED CUDGEL *absorbs another blow. His cup is refilled.*)

RED CUDGEL: What's going on here?

WHITE PAPER FAN: We are afraid that the bandit authorities will want to deport you. A pity Night Brother couldn't arrange more discreet treatment for you.

NIGHT BROTHER: Elder Brother's life was my priority. You were losing blood. I had to get immediate help.

WHITE PAPER FAN: This matter was even reported in the newspapers . . .
(*There is a short silence. All faces are turned away.*)
From now on, the policy will be to divide territories and live in peace with our competitors.

RED CUDGEL: Live in peace! Are you a child? They'll do a deal today and swallow us tomorrow.

WHITE PAPER FAN: With respect, I think we shall benefit greatly. You see, your errors were not only in the military sphere. For example, this runner you ordered washed was innocent. He was set up by this 'useful' man of yours, one of your new recruits.

RED CUDGEL: He's already been washed?

WHITE PAPER FAN: You will remember how I advised against hasty action. This could do us untold harm.
(NIGHT BROTHER *goes to top up* RED CUDGEL's *tea once more. With a sweep of his hand,* RED CUDGEL *knocks the teapot off the table. It smashes on the floor.*)

NIGHT BROTHER: The man's wife has interesting connections. Her father is Tang Cheung Ching. From Dah Ling village.
(RED CUDGEL's *head is bowed.*)

WHITE PAPER FAN: The recruit, Fok, can be made use of. They want revenge for their men killed by us.

RED CUDGEL: The waiter's widow must be supported. You

must promise me this . . .
(WHITE PAPER FAN *is nodding.* RED CUDGEL *has in effect conceded the leadership.*)
WHITE PAPER FAN: It will be done . . . a small regular payment could be sent, perhaps through our Amsterdam contacts. But, gentlemen, let's not be gloomy. This is a celebration. We are conferring on Elder Brother the elevated Double Flower prefix . . .
(*He takes a badge and pins it to* RED CUDGEL's *lapel.*)
Tonight he assumes four three eight status. Good fortune in Hong Kong. Let's all drink to that. Yum Sing!
(*The others raise their glasses. There is a ragged chorus of toasts.* RED CUDGEL *makes no acknowledgement.*)
Cut to:

The takeaway.
It is dawn. The kitchen. LILY *sits in a chair dozing. In shot is the telephone.*
MUI *comes into the kitchen in her dressing-gown. She carries a blanket which she tucks round her sister.*
Cut to:

The bedroom.
LILY *is rummaging through Chen's pockets for a sign, a clue to his disappearance.*
From the pocket of a jacket she retrieves the pebble she once presented to Chen on Margate beach.
The associations of the object are too much for her. Clutching the stone, she makes for the bed where she sits and weeps.
Cut to:

An hour later. We are looking into the bedroom from the doorway.
LILY *has crawled under a blanket which she has drawn up over her head. She is awake, but silent.*
A reverse shot shows that we are looking into the room from MAN KEE's *point of view.*
He stands by the half-open door, his eyes round and staring.

MUI *appears. We see her hands on* MAN KEE's *shoulders as she leads him away.*
   Slow mix to:

The takeaway.
   Months later. The kitchen. A pram is in shot.
   Watched by MUI, LO, MAN KEE, GRANDPA *and*
CONSTANTINIDES, LILY *is tearing open an envelope.*
   She gives a shout of triumph.
LILY: Look! Mui, look!
   (*Ten ten-pound notes are spread across the table.*)
   I knew! I knew he wouldn't let us down.
   (CONSTANTINIDES *takes the envelope. There is no letter inside. He examines the stamp.*)
CONSTANTINIDES: It's from Holland, Amsterdam . . .
LILY: He must have a restaurant job there.
MUI: What makes you so sure Ah Chen sent the money?
LILY: Who else is going to send it? He knew the business wasn't making enough. Not enough to look after Man Kee as he gets older. He's a true father to make a sacrifice like this . . .
MUI: But why isn't there a letter . . .?
LILY: Don't you see? He knew I would try to stop him going, and he knows I would tell him to come back . . .
   (MUI *is about to dispute this, but she changes her mind.*)
MUI: Ah . . . wonderful, Lily, wonderful . . . and I've got some good news too . . . Ah . . . I'm going to get married . . .
LILY: Married?
MUI: To Mr Lo . . .
LILY: To Mr Lo? Well . . . that's good, good. What a surprise, what a . . . a happy occasion.
   (*The sisters embrace.*)
MUI: And we're going to start a business. A fish-and-chip shop.
LILY: Mui!
   Cut to:

(LILY *stands outside the house watching* MUI *and* LO *walk away pushing the pram. Lay over the following:*)

82

MUI: I want to ask you something, Younger Sister. It's the thing closest to my heart. Come and live with my family . . .
LILY: I'll be fine, you'll see . . .
MUI: There'll be a place for you in our house whenever you want it, Lily.
LILY: I'll be fine.
(GRANDPA *and* MAN KEE *are by the front door, watching* LILY. *All three go indoors.*)
Cut to:

The garden. Many weeks later.
   The afternoon light is failing. The sky is sombre.
   LILY *walks slowly and reflectively down the garden.*
   Her voice is close, intimate.
LILY: (*Voice over*) My dearest one, I am so glad you are safe. Your money arrives regularly now, and it makes me proud to think how we Chinese know how to look after our own. I know that one day soon you will send me an address . . .
(*At this point we shift our angle. A long, elevated shot shows us the whole garden and a great sweep of city beyond.* LILY *is a diminutive figure. She is just arriving at the bottom of the garden where she stops.*)
(*Voice over*) I love you dearly, more and more each day, and I look forward to the time when you return which I know in my heart you will. In the meantime I want you to know that I feel strong, like a warrior, and light, so light . . .
(LILY *adopts the stylized pose of the fighter, taught to her by her father. She remains in this pose for some time.*
Wedding song, as we pan across the city.)